HER

GARRY DISHER

HER

hachette
AUSTRALIA

The writing of this novel was assisted by the Australian Government through the Australia Council for the Arts, its arts funding and advisory body.

Published in Australia and New Zealand in 2017
by Hachette Australia
(an imprint of Hachette Australia Pty Limited)
Level 17, 207 Kent Street, Sydney NSW 2000
www.hachette.com.au

10 9 8 7 6 5 4 3 2 1

National Library of Australia
Cataloguing-in-Publication data

Disher, Garry, 1949– author.
Her/Garry Disher.

ISBN: 978 0 7336 3854 1 (pbk)
Girls – Australia – History – Fiction.
Women – Australia – History – Fiction.
Suspense fiction.

Cover design by Astred Hicks
Cover image courtesy Craig Jewell Photography
Text design by Bookhouse, Sydney
Typeset in 12.5/20 pt Adobe Garamond Pro by Bookhouse, Sydney
Reading group notes by Robyn Sheahan-Bright
Printed and bound in Australia by McPherson's Printing Group

to the memory of
Lettie Disher
1924–2016

1909

out in that country

OUT IN THAT COUNTRY THE SUN SMEARED THE SKY AND nothing ever altered, except that one day a scrap man came by with his wife, who had cost him twelve shillings once upon a time, and a wispy girl, who had cost him ten.

The people of the hut heard them first, the clop two three four of hooves, the creature-in-torment shriek of an axle and a mad symphony of tocking and rattling. They froze. Then, from the scrub line, came a bony horse, a wagon hung with pots and pans, a dog panting along in the lurching shade and three faces, dusty and gaunt.

'Whoa!' said the man, spying the hut and hauling on the reins.

The dust settled over the clearing. The pots and pans fell silent on their hooks. The horse hung its head and the dog belly-flopped onto the dirt.

After a while a child appeared, wearing a flour-bag dress and slipping soundlessly from beneath a sulky parked broken-backed in a collar of grass. Other figures joined her, the odds and ends of a used-up family, materialising from the hut, a barn, a post-and-rail fence and the tricky corners of the mallee scrub. Count them: a mother, a father and eleven children, ranging from a baby on a hip to a boy whose voice had broken, all staring at the apparition.

'Bring out your bottles,' rasped the scrap man from his wagon seat, 'your rags, tin, copper and brass.'

He was a dapper man, his hat at a jaunty angle, but the family might not have heard him, so mute were they, without suspicion, hope or awe. They were too numerous, too hungry, too far from the nearest town. Out here the sky pressed down and the dirt hemmed them in. No outlander like the scrap man could save them.

Acknowledging this, the farmer exchanged a look with his wife:

Do we have anything worth selling?

No.

'Saucepans mended,' tried the scrap man, appealing to the wife. 'Knives sharpened.'

She gestured at her threadbare existence. 'Ain't got no money,' she whispered.

But the scrap man's attention had wandered. He'd spotted the daughters. So many of them clustered together, ankles grimy and showing out of their dresses, yet each as beautiful as a wildflower. He jumped down from the wagon. He gave an elaborate yawn. He stretched the kinks in his spine.

No one was fooled. The older girls took a step back.

Undeterred, the scrap man fished a tin and papers from the breast pocket of his gappy shirt. He rolled a miserly cigarette. 'Smoke?' he suggested, fixing on the farmer.

The two men ambled away to the barn, trailing ash and business. The minutes lengthened. The wife, overcome with shyness, ducked back into the hut and one by one her sons and daughters drifted away, leaving only the little ones, who continued to stare.

And so much to stare at. The three-year-old drank in the enormous wheels, a brief shudder in the hide of the horse, the woman and the girl motionless on a wooden bench . . . and the painted stars, gold, silver, speckling the canvas hood.

Presently she sensed the scrap man at her side. His long fingers flicked up and down her limbs, squeezing, testing. 'This one,' he said.

She took no notice. She continued to marvel, a tawny-headed, scab-kneed, fearless scrap of a girl. But she occupied an indeterminate position among her brothers and sisters. Her name was scarcely known or remembered. All in all, she was worth less than the nine shillings and sixpence the scrap man had counted into her father's hand.

1913

the stony acres

NAMES HAD NO CURRENCY IN THE SCRAP MAN'S FAMILY. Whether roaming door to door in the back country, or lingering here on their stony acres, the woman and the two girls were You. Their ages were immaterial, too. What mattered to the scrap man was, would they bend their backs to the chores he'd set them? He was He, Him.

The little one slept in the grassy dirt between the wagon wheels, the big girl under the canopy above, and the woman with the man in the tent. But he liked to come visiting Big Girl. In the night the little one heard strange yelps and moans and Big Girl's whimpers overhead, the wagon tray softly protesting. Until one day there was going to be a baby and the visits ceased.

This morning You was woken by the dawn birds, light leaking in and the wagon tilting above her head as one heavy foot after the other came clumping down the steps. Reaching the ground, Big Girl groaned and put a hand to the small of her back. She turned, trudged a short distance, and presently there was a squirting onto the dirt. She shuffled back to the wagon and stopped there, and You sensed her tremulous contemplation of the lowest wagon step, so high above the ground.

So You crawled out. The sun was an eyebrow of red and yellow on the distant hilltops. She tapped Big Girl's shoulder: 'Swap?'

Big Girl slumped, all energy spent. The baby kicked in her belly and all she wanted was to sleep. She grunted yes, for the family had little need of sentences, and crawled into her new cave. Sounds then of the mattress accommodating her unfamiliar shape, straw scratching and shifting.

You climbed aboard the wagon and stretched out on the big girl's mattress – like hers, a few sugar bags stitched together and stuffed with straw. But this mattress was also full of knots and hollows that twisted her hip and knuckled her spine. And the pillow, a trouser leg stuffed with grass, was lumpy, stale and damp.

She stared up at the underside of the canvas hood. Here and there the gold and silver stars showed through but their magic was long gone from her life. She tried to read the other shapes formed by the wrinkles, stains and repairs. A dog with a curled tail. A bird with a pointy beak. A castle on a misty mountain. This was her second castle: her first had been a picture in a magazine long ago, before it was snatched from her grasp and used to set a campfire on some winding track.

It was no good; she couldn't sleep. In the brief holidays between his tantrums, the scrap man was known to say, 'Pull a long face and carry on,' and that's what You said now, 'Pull a long face and carry on,' as she jumped from the wagon to the ground.

Ducking between the wheels, she looked for her flour-bag dress. There it was, trapped under Big Girl's legs. She tugged gently, not waking her, and pulled it on.

Then on bare feet she skirted behind the tent, where the scrap man snored and the woman, his wife, lay silent beside him. The ground was night-cool and full of small, stabbing stones. Reaching the site of their partially built hut, she jumped in fright. Some creature had stirred near the cleared patch of dirt floors and shin-high stone walls, the piles of stolen planks and roofing iron. A rabbit, a bush rat, a snake, a mouse?

Untying the dog, she hurried on to the edge of the creek. Here was the horse in his pen, a handful of rotten posts looped together with fencing wire filched from the neighbours. He snorted and flicked his tail to see You and the dog, and his ribcage hide shuddered as she murmured into his ear and tied a rope around his neck. Talking to her animals was the most conversation You ever had and, still talking, she led the horse and the dog along the bank to the first of her rabbit traps.

THIS WAS HER daily routine: up at first light, fetch the horse, check her fifteen traps, kill any rabbits still alive, haul the carcasses back to camp, skin and gut them, check again after lunch, and again at dinnertime, and if she were lucky she'd be in bed before midnight. The creek banks were polka-dotted with burrows. The rabbits kept coming. You told a joke the family failed to laugh at, for they never laughed: 'I had to push away rabbits to set my traps!'

Eight rabbits this morning, same as yesterday morning, and six yesterday afternoon and four last night. They just kept coming, silly enough to hop through the grass and into the blood-and-rust-stained metal jaws. Some would die, the living she killed with a whip-crack action that snapped their spines. She spoke sternly to the dog, 'Keep back,' for the rabbits represented money in the scrap man's pockets.

After resetting the last trap and hooking the last carcass to the seven slung across the horse, You retraced her steps along the bank. The creek bed was dry. She liked it best in full flood and when pools persisted, home to the yabbies she'd catch with a string, a tree-bark grub and a wire-mesh scoop. She was hungry – she could smell wood smoke and frying meat on the wind – but paused before making the last descent from the upper bank to the hollow below, where breakfast was waiting. Instead, she took a moment to check if the Education or the Social or a policeman or priest were lurking. The scrap man had beaten it into her often enough: 'Run and hide, you see any strangers, all right? If they catch you, don't say nothing. Act simple-minded, hear?'

No strangers, only Wife at the fire in its stone hearth, jiggling the frying pan, swinging the billy of tea around her head, so it was safe for You to come down the slope, the horse at her side. Wife, without looking at her, said, 'You, do them skins first, hear?'

•

You was a fast worker, faster and neater than the scrap man, Wife or Big Girl. Flick, flick, flick went the knife, until the skin was ready to be peeled from the carcass like a sock from your foot. Then she stretched each skin on a loop of stolen fencing wire and hung it on the horse pen to cure. When the time came, Wife would sell them to Anderson's the skin merchant in return for a few coins. The woman was sly with that money or the scrap man would drink it all away.

That left the carcasses, and they were cash money, too. With one long slice of the blade, You would make a belly slit, reach in her little hand and scoop out the innards, toss them into the grass for the dog. She always gutted the rabbits imagining the scrap man with his gizzards spilled in the dirt. She washed and shook dry and stacked each pale pink-and-grey bunch of meat, muscle and bone, ready for Wife to cart to the butcher in town.

You ate her breakfast finally, dizzy with hunger and fatigue. The sun warmed the dirt and her limbs, and the colours all about her were red, yellow and brown. Sometimes light glinted at her from the pebbles and dead grass, but it was never a diamond, only a chip of flint. No gold hereabouts, either, but gold had brought them to this place, the scrap man buying the stony acres after chancing upon a nugget the size of a tin cup last year. Or rather, after Wife and the two girls had chanced upon it, panning and fossicking along a different creek on a different back road while he snored under the wagon.

Sleep was all that You wanted now. She stretched out in the dirt beside the dog and presently the scrap man came along and kicked her in the hip. 'You. Up.'

She blinked awake. He loomed over her, robbing the sunlight. Here on the stony acres he was not a fine-looking door-to-door salesman in a neat, threadbare suit and cocky hat but a whiskery thug in work clothes, though he did no work. 'Up,' he growled, one of his pinched-looking smokes bobbing in the corner of his mouth. Another kick. His boots were held together with wire but the steel tip still worked.

You stood, brushing off dirt and dead grass. From the stillness and silence and absences she understood that the woman had taken the buggy-load of carcasses to the butcher. Big Girl sat stunned beside the breakfast fire, which had been reduced to one smoking coal.

'Get a move on,' growled the scrap man.

You followed him to a patch of ground roofed by a filthy canvas square roped to a couple of trees. Milk-powder tins were heaped there, lengths of fencing wire and pliers and tinsnips and metal files. He grunted, gestured, shuffled off towards the tent.

Knowing she was expected to make toasting forks, You scooted in and reached for the first scrap of fencing wire. She cut a short length, sharpened each end with a file, bent it into a U shape. Then she cut a longer piece. One end would be the handle, the other the third prong. She hadn't the hand-strength for twisting the pieces together. The scrap man would do that, about all he ever did. Reading the sky, the seasons, the scrap man's moods and grunts, You understood that they were getting ready for their long annual roaming of the back roads, the wagon hung with goods for sale. Last year a farmer's wife told them, 'That there oven mitt you sold me didn't last a week.'

You finished her filing. Her arms and wrists ached, but it was not yet time to run her trap line again, so she fitted wire handles to a couple of milk-powder tins. The scrap man called them billies, for billy tea. They wouldn't last a week.

Even so, the wire was stiff and nasty and a sharp end sliced through the ball of her thumb. She put it to her mouth. The blood tasted like iron. She pulled it out, examined the cut. A line of tiny red beads appeared. She had a memory then of falling down and scraping her knee, of soft arms around her. Not Wife's arms, or Big Girl's, that was for sure – so whose arms, making it all better? A woman in a dream, or a long-ago woman, not a woman in her life now.

•

SHE WAS STILL in that dream when the scrap man appeared, hissing at her, 'You shut your gob.'

Startled, she saw that he'd swapped his greasy hat for the good one and dragged on a jacket, and now was scurrying across the stony ground to Big Girl, who sat on a tree stump turning empty flour bags into aprons and tablecloths. 'Move!'

He hauled her slow ponderous shape across the ground to the wagon and shoved her under it before racing back to where she'd been working. Gathering the empty flour bags, scissors and balls of thread as if it were strange stuff, he gazed around in a panic and came running to You in the canvas shelter. Thrusting it all at her feet, he snarled, 'Keep your gob shut.'

She'd already worked that out. She'd already heard the clop of hooves and the creak of saddle leather and understood that it was too late for her to hide from the horseman riding in from the horizon.

•

FROM ON HIGH he said, 'Hello, little girl.'

You said nothing. She stared up at him blankly. His saddle gleamed, his boots. She'd never seen a shirt or teeth so crisply white. A thick, luxuriant moustache and long, slender hands on the reins. His eyes were hard on her, assessing but not cruel, which confused her: the scrap man was always saying, 'They're shits, them lot, you can't trust the cunts.'

You tensed. The man from the Education or the Social leaned down and said, 'Shouldn't you be at school?'

She said nothing.

The scrap man came sauntering up, a man with nothing to hide. 'Don't waste your breath. She's feeble in the head.'

He'd removed his hat out of respect to a gentleman, and now his blockish, unshaven cheeks and bleary eyes were revealed to the world. 'She can't talk.'

The horseman swung his gaze back and forth. 'Oh.'

'Won't say boo to a goose.'

The fine man dismounted and removed his own hat and offered a handshake. The scrap man stared at it dumbfounded but, quick to know what side his bread was buttered on, closed his mouth with a click of ill-fitting teeth, smiled, wiped his fingers on the slope of his trousers and said, 'Pleased to make your acquaintance.'

The men shook, but then the horseman said, 'I understand you have two school-age daughters?'

The scrap man's eyes turned skittish, not alighting on anything but possible escape routes, until he managed to recover, replace his hat and nod at You. 'Only her. She got no brains.'

'We've had reports of an older child,' the horseman said. 'About twelve, thirteen?'

The scrap man held his chin in his hand in a parody of deep thinking and dawning realisation. 'That would of been me sister's girl. Up from Melbourne for a visit and that.'

'She doesn't live with you?'

'Got no room for another mouth,' the scrap man said, gesturing at his kingdom.

'Is your wife around, Mr . . . ?'

'She's gone to town, shopping and that. Don't know when she'll be back.'

'To be clear, there is you, your wife and this little girl?'

'That's right,' the scrap man said. In his cringing way he added, 'You from the Education?'

'That's correct. The school year has started and it is incumbent upon me to ensure that all school-age children are attending classes.'

'Me daughter's feeble-minded.'

The fine horseman swung his attention to You, seated in the dirt. She saw herself as he saw her, a thin, gaping dress and grubby feet and grimy hands and knots in her hair, all certain proof of feeble-mindedness.

And then he was bending his handsome head and with his glistening smile and clear enunciation he said, 'Hello there, what . . . is . . . your . . . name?'

As if You were deaf in addition to not being right in the head. But she was struck by the question. She'd never been asked it before. She thought she must have had a name, once upon a time, but it had been forgotten. What was it? Who knew it? She opened her mouth to answer and the scrap man said, in a loud rush, 'Won't do you no good.'

Unwitnessed by the Education he glared at You, his eyes promising kicks, pinches and his whipping belt buckle on her bare behind if she spoke. He said to the gentleman, 'Anyfink else I can do for you?'

The Education smiled no, settled his hat on his head, shook hands again and, before You knew it, he was gone, his horse cantering neatly, raising puffs of dust. She stared at his receding back and felt utterly sad. Then she stared at the scraps of wire and sewing rags, avoiding the scrap man's gaze. The slightest thing would inflame him, bring hell upon her head.

Looking down like that, she saw that ants were busy in the dirt.

'Rain,' the scrap man said, also staring at the busyness of the ants.

You hoped he'd wander off but he stood there and she kept an eye on his kicking boot. 'I didn't say nuffink.'

Even saying that might be sufficient to inflame him, but all he said was, 'Do your traps.'

Having the sense not to point out that his wife had taken the horse to town, You scrambled to her feet and trudged towards the creek as if willing, the dog hard at her heels. She clambered up the main bank and turned to look down upon the camp and, sure enough, the scrap man was crawling into the tent, where his sherry bottles beckoned.

•

HERE ON THE upper bank, there were more busy ants. She squatted for a while, watching, her chin and cheeks cupped by her hands while the dog collapsed with a squeaky yawn. The ants streamed from holes that were like pores in the skin of the world. You bewitched herself, crouching and peering like that, not moving a muscle, nothing moving anywhere apart from the ants. She lost herself to her dreams, the sun warming her bones. Ants busy in the dirt meant that rain was on the way, so the scrap man always said. You shuddered, hating it that he'd slipped into her head. Could anyone believe a word he said? She stared at the limitless dome of sky and all she saw was a fat white cotton ball far off over a blue-grey line of hills.

What would it be to run now, see what beheld her on the other side of those hills? An unbidden thought, but not a new one, and as usual she trembled, hugging herself protectively, certain the scrap man had the power to read her mind.

As she stared out over the world, a watery image came creeping across the flats, resolving as Wife, the buggy and the weary horse. There were shop-bought boxes and bags behind the buggy seat, and she knew she was expected to help unload. He'd be no help. He'd be snoring.

She uncoiled from the dirt and leaped and skittered downslope to the dead campfire, reaching it as Wife did. The woman grunted, which meant: *Feed and water the horse.* You complied, sensing great exhaustion in the horse. He was damp, trembling, weakened from the round trip, hauling the buggy.

When that was done, she returned to Wife and muttered, 'Horse isn't too good.'

Wife bristled, as though You had dared to criticise. She grunted, jerked her head at the buggy, meaning, *Help unload.*

You dragged the first bag of flour to the edge, staggered with it across the yard and stowed it under a tarp stretched between a couple of trees. 'We're gonna need a storeroom,' the scrap man kept saying, but where was it? You made several trips back and forth. Sugar, tins of powdered milk, cans of soup – not that she got to eat soup very often.

She said nothing, just staggered with her burdens as if she were as feeble-minded as they all said she was, yet keeping a secret eye on the woman. Wife, dressed in a pinny over a long gown of stitched-together hessian sacks, was running her fingers in a musical tinkle through pennies, ha'pennies, sixpences and shillings in her pinny pocket. Easy to know what she was thinking. She was thinking: *Please, God, don't let him get his hands on the rabbit money* or it would all be gone on beer, sherry and the kinds of women who smile at shearers, railway gangers and travelling salesmen.

The coins sang. You, continuing to spy as she unloaded the buggy, knew what Wife would do next. She'd hand some coins to the scrap man, to calm his mad rantings in the afternoons of their lives, and conceal the rest. The hiding place was a tattered cardboard school case where Wife and Big Girl stowed the washed and folded rags for their monthly bleedings. The scrap man would not in a million years consider sticking his hand under the lid of that case.

You staggered with the last of the shopping, a bag of sugar clasped to her chest. It slipped down her tiny frame to the dust and Wife grunted and lifted and helped stack it. Wasted by the effort, the woman gave a rattling cough, spat an evil stream of tobacco into the dirt, then grimaced, revealing a graveyard of chipped green teeth. She had a face full of craters, too, and her ribs had been cracked more than once. She didn't know that. She only knew that each time she recovered she was a little more twisted when she laboured at her chores, gradually favouring one side over the other a little more. She said, one day when the scrap man was away, the womenfolk snatching at the chance to talk, 'He got me on me fif birfday.' She thought she was maybe twenty years old. She couldn't count past twenty. He'd put his thing in her but a baby hadn't come, so he bought Big Girl. Then, more the merrier, he bought You.

You, awed to be the subject of a story, asked, 'How old am I?'

Wife concentrated hard. 'I fink you was free. I fink you're six now.'

•

THE SHOPPING UNLOADED, Wife said, 'Do your traps.'

You skirted around the snoring tent and past the wood and iron piled beside the house site, one eye open for snakes. None this afternoon, but there was a skink, a tiny brown quicksilver creature looking at her. She crouched, curious, and time went by, the pair exchanging unblinking stares. You blinked first and the skink *flick flick* vanished into a gap between the stolen garden stones reserved for the chimney.

After that, You was absorbed by a wedge-tailed eagle. She watched it float on the currents above the flats on the other side of the creek. Squadrons of small birds streamed madly up from the trees, screeching *heed* to each other and gamely warning off the eagle, which sideslipped away, revealing a vector of sky and a second eagle, further away. By now, You hadn't even reached the first of her rabbit traps and the afternoon had disappeared into a smear of sunset to light her way home. Five rabbits this time.

•

HE WAS UP, sitting on a log by the fire, being fed rabbit stew by Big Girl and Wife, both hovering ready to jump to it while keeping clear of his boots and fists. When he noticed You, his eyes fixed on her drunkenly, red-streaked and moist.

'*You*,' he thundered.

She jumped.

He jerked his head to indicate Wife. 'She reckons we need a new horse.'

You glanced at Wife, who was wringing her hands as if to say: *Please back me up*. You said firmly, 'Are we goin' on another sellin' trip soon?'

'What of it?'

What did he think? Weeks, months on the road, the horse dragging them all over the countryside in the wagon? She said, 'It'll kill him, pullin' the wagon. We do need another horse, a strong one.'

The scrap man looked away, dribbling a few filthy words. Another horse meant having to spend money, which always got him riled. To make himself feel better, he turned to You and snarled, 'Where you been, anyway?'

'Traps.'

'Time do you call this? You been wool-gathering again?'

He liked to accuse her of daydreaming, twiddling her thumbs. Right now he was saying she shouldn't think about a feed or sleep until she'd skinned and dressed the carcasses, so she went to work. She strung up the first rabbit, made her shallow cuts around the forefeet, the ears and anus, and peeled off the skin in one smooth motion. Spread the pelt on a wire, then turned to the body, cut out the gizzards, washed and cleaned it all away. In the meantime the scrap man had fallen asleep in the dirt. Big Girl darted in, fished a greasy grey blob from the stew pot and handed it to You. You grunted her thanks and gobbled it up, and that's how the woman and the girls survived their days with the scrap man, little kindnesses exchanged, grunted thanks, protective acts.

•

AND THEN IT was time for You to set out for the last trap run of the day, the dog tied up for he got skittish at night. A kerosene lantern swung from her hand, casting a weak pool of yellow light around her feet.

Just as she reached the horse pen, Wife said in the darkness behind her, 'Leave the traps till mornin'. I want plums, strawb'ries, termarters.'

You turned, took two tin buckets from the woman, headed across the dry creek bed, her path lit by the lantern. She climbed the bank and soon the camp was far behind her and she was passing by her traps and climbing through a rusty wire fence. Her destination was a homestead with a hedged-in stone house and several outlying sheds, haystacks, water tanks and sheep yards. Lit by the tricky shadows cast by the sorry light, she picked her way across the stubbled paddocks patrolled by the eagles. Stones twisted her ankles, star thistles pierced her calves. When she neared the farmhouse, she turned off the lantern, hearing the scrap man in her head: 'Use your brains.'

Now the world about her was blurry under a sliver of moon glow. Reaching a gap in the hedge that divided the rear of the house from the various sheds, she waited, listened. Window light illuminated the back veranda and nearby paths and garden beds. Nothing had changed since last time. Roses close to the house, vegetables and berries in beds further out, with a scattering of peach, plum and apricot trees.

Movement at a window. She froze. Then the shape was gone again, but she could hear music, someone at a piano, trilling up and down the scales. People in a house, with their own lights and ways, it was unimaginable, beyond her grasp.

You waited and here came the farm dog, a kelpie full of wet, snuffling joy, slobbering over her fingers, his tail whipping her thigh. She squatted to hug his neck and whispered, 'You can smell my dog, can't you?' as she scratched behind his ears until he collapsed in the dirt, offering his belly. She rubbed him and he was ecstatic. He didn't bark; he'd never barked when You came stealing by in the night. But he'd bark at a possum, a swagman, a fox or his own shadow.

You made for the plum tree and picked judiciously, a plum here, a plum there, so that her thievery might go unnoticed. When the first bucket was half full, she topped it up with strawberries from a raised bed. Jam-making tomorrow, jars of it to sell along with toasting forks in the back country farms and towns when the time came. She ate one plum and some of the strawberries, she couldn't help it.

Yet as she filled the buckets the glowing window beckoned, so warm and yellow and full of promise. She set the buckets in the dirt and crept towards the house, her heart hammering. Onto the veranda, the glassy concrete still warm from the afternoon sun, a balm to her pricked and bruised feet. Then, half-crouched, she crossed to that window and hooked her nose over the sill, breathing shallowly.

•

A GIRL WITH plaited hair tied with ribbons sat on a rug on floorboards beside a bed. She was humming, the sound reaching You plainly through a gap between window and sill.

Too many things to take in at once, so You gave her attention to one detail, then another, for they were all marvels to her. Beyond the girl a white door sat ajar in a papered wall, flowers repeated oppressively up, down and sideways. You could almost feel those walls pressing in on her, so she switched her attention to the floor, where a thick, blue, tasselled rug sailed on a sea of gleaming dark boards. Now the girl, cross-legged on the rug: shiny brown hair fastened with yellow ribbons, the ties coming adrift where they sat on the shoulders of a pretty yellow dress.

Finally, the doll's house.

You stared, lost in wonder. Such inexpressible beauty in the pale blue walls with darker blue window frames, the bright red door, the tiled roof with two chimneys. And, as You watched, the girl leaned forward, tipped back the roof, opened the front wall, sat back on her bare heels again. There, revealed to the world, were tiny chairs and wardrobes and beds and people. The girl hummed. She reached in, placed a bed beneath a window, sat back, mused, reached in and set a chair before a fireplace.

Yet something was wrong. The humming grew agitated, words breaking in: 'Sing a song of sixpence . . . I will not say it again, young lady . . . Now look what you've made me do . . . Four-and-twenty blackbirds . . .'

This went on. You flicked her gaze away from the doll's house as if the room might explain the girl's mood. The bed was a high structure dressed in pink chenille tight as a drum. A glum wardrobe sat in the corner, so dark it absorbed light. A chest of drawers with a white embroidered cloth atop it, a chair, a floral dressing-gown hooked to the back of the door.

'Another think coming!' shrieked the girl, and she plucked the piano from the upper floor of the doll's house and flung it against the wardrobe. It bounced off and landed beside her knee. She stared down at it, her bottom lip in a sulk. The scrap man didn't like it if you got the sulks. He'd beat it out of his women, and You watched to see what would happen to the girl now. But no one came. The girl plucked out an armchair and threw it at the wall. 'Hate you,' she said.

Why, if you had a beautiful doll's house, would you throw a tantrum? You was frightened and troubled and slid off the veranda, withdrawing into the evening shadows. She had never thrown a tantrum, barely knew what being cross felt like. Only the scrap man was allowed to show his temper – and sometimes the woman, when she smacked You or Big Girl in order to save herself from him. Why had the girl got cross? Was it allowed?

You crept around to the vegetable patch and picked enough tomatoes to fill the second bucket. Fruit for jam, tomatoes for chutney, relish and sauce. Hurrying now, she made for the gap in the hedge, pausing to survey the stony paddock in the moonlight. But ritual demanded that she hug the dog first. She'd hug that dog for hours, all of her life, if she were allowed to. If she couldn't be hugged or patted then at least she could do the hugging and patting.

It mended her.

•

THE NEXT MORNING, You returned from her trap run to find the scrap man waiting at the pen. He'd given himself an approximate shave, some stubble at the hinge of his jaw, blood dots here and there. He wore his town shirt with the yellow armpits, his old suit coat and best hat, an ever-present cigarette in the corner of his mouth.

Without a word, he tipped the rabbits – eight this morning – into the dirt and yanked the reins from her grasp, hurting the horse, hurting her palm. He paid no attention but pulled the horse to the mounting stump, where he heaved a saddle over the bony, bowed spine, cinching it tightly before rolling himself aboard. One day the womenfolk had seen him tip right over the horse and land with a whump on the other side. They hadn't dared laugh. Hell to pay if he caught them laughing. But they roared with it once he was out of sight.

As You retrieved her rabbits, the scrap man rode across the yard to the campfire, where jam and relish bubbled in iron pots. He leaned from the saddle, stuck out his hand. Wife, fishing reluctantly in her pinny, tipped coins into it. Then man and horse headed for the road. The horse, slow, metronomic, ignored the man's heels frantically stabbing its hide, seeking speed.

Did the horse have a name? You had never considered the matter. He didn't need a name in her dealings with him. He was simply an essence of bigness, warmth, tough pelt and snorts and liquid eyes gazing trustingly at her.

Poor horse.

•

THE EIGHT CARCASSES skinned and gutted, You tumbled the innards into the dirt for the dog. But he merely lay belly-down and stared, his tail beating weakly when she implored him to eat. 'Not hungry?'

Watching him from the corner of her eye, she washed the blood and goo from her hands and joined Wife and Big Girl at the cooking pots. Wife gave her a chopping board, a knife and last night's plums. Her grunt said, *You know what to do.*

The blade sliced soundlessly through the flesh, tapping as it met the board, over and over again. A pot of strawberries and sugar went *plop plop plop* on the fire. Coals crackled. Chests breathed in and out. Fabric scraped with each breath and each arm movement as Wife, Big Girl and You cut, scraped, measured, poured, stirred.

The women's fear and anxiety began to ebb. No scrap man to pinch, cuff or berate them. This was a time to treasure. Mostly they worked in silence, but might stretch the kinks in their backs, or yawn, or sigh, and exchange shy smiles. Once when Big Girl rubbed the ache from her spine, she caught You looking at her cross-eyed, a plum stone in each nostril. She got the giggles. Then the baby moved and the others placed their hands on her belly, their lips parted in awe. To celebrate, Wife made hot jam sandwiches, which they washed down with sugary tea. The world was at peace.

And then Big Girl glanced at the sky, gauging the time. She said, 'Bet he's at the pub.'

Wife looked frightened. Big Girl had broken the spell, reminding them that after a day at the pub the scrap man was apt to break their bones. She said curtly, 'Get on with it.'

The wife in a temper could be as bad as the scrap man, so You hunched her shoulders to avoid notice. To look busy, she slid plum slices into a pot, added sugar and a little water, stirred. Time passed. The jams and chutneys cooled. Using a dipper, she ladled jam into jars, sealed them, stowed them away from the ants. But yes, the spell was broken. The sun was sliding towards the horizon and the scrap man could be heard approaching on the old nag.

•

HE ARRIVED SOBER with a whole window, glass and frame, digging into the neck of the horse.

Pulling up at the house site, he said, 'Don't just stand there.'

His wife ran to him and Big Girl waddled across the stony yard. You took her time, struck by the curious shapes etched by man, horse and window against the evening sky. A collection of angles that did not fit with one another. Lumpy roundness, twiggy limbs, the square window a kind of tilted sail. But then she saw the state of the horse. Had he even been fed or watered? The poor creature hung his head, trembling uncontrollably, flecked with foam, striped with cuts where the scrap man had heeled him, no doubt screaming, 'Gee up, you bloody black whore,' like he always did. She laid her hand on the horse's moist flank, feeling the bones underneath.

The scrap man glared at her, astounded. 'What do you think you're doing? Help, blast you.'

He handed the window to Wife and the two girls, warning, 'If you break the flaming thing . . .'

Hell to pay, that's what.

Had he stolen the window? That's how he acquired most things. Had he bought it with his pub money? No. Such restraint was unheard of.

The womenfolk struggled. The window was lopsidedly heavy and wanted to smash to the ground. It dug into their hands and pulled on their shoulders and You could feel how rotten the wooden frame was, flaky, chipped and worn away. Old paint chips dug into her palms. Cobweb traceries in the corners. And the glass when it reflected the setting sun was smeared with handprints and dust.

The scrap man climbed down to help at last. 'Termorrer,' he said, taking the window and setting one edge on the ground, 'we do more work on the house.'

Then he lifted the window, staggered with it to his pile of timber and iron, set it down again. He always made a big production of anything he did, as if he faced impossible odds and deserved adulation afterwards. You had seen it all before. She turned her back on him and led the horse to his pen, stroking, murmuring. She gave him hay and oats, fetched water from a muddy spring in the creek bed. The horse showed scant interest in the food, but he slurped at the water and snorted his thanks at You with a wild rolling of his eyes, a nuzzling of his long nose against her ribcage.

She remembered the dog. He didn't come when she called.

•

SHE FOUND HIM at dawn, in the dirt beside the new window, his neck stretched out and his eyes blankly staring at a couple of pebbles. He looked sunken and desiccated in death and her skin crept in revulsion. But that made her feel traitorous, disloyal to his memory. Confused, she backed away and ran to the pen to collect the horse.

Six rabbits, and when You had finished skinning and gutting, she told Wife about the dog.

'Don't want it stinkin' the place out,' was all Wife said.

So You dragged the body into the bush. She thought of burying him, but the ground was more stone than soil.

•

BREAKFAST WAS A thin smear of strawberry jam on a slab of stale bread. Warm stale water. One bruised and split plum she'd saved from yesterday.

Of course the scrap man slept the morning away and emerged with grand plans for the hut.

'The dog died,' You said.

He waved that away. 'One less mouth to feed,' he said. 'Until I put sheep on this place there's no point getting another mutt. Now, this is what I have in mind.'

He indicated which of the dirt floors would be the kitchen, the sitting room, the main bedroom, the bedroom for Big Girl and her baby. He showed them where he wanted the chimney and hearth. 'All we need is more stones and mud to glue them together,' he said.

Easy for him to say, You thought. He never does the heavy lifting.

•

THE DAYS DRAGGED, the scrap man screeching, 'Put your backs into it,' flicking his ash at them. They hauled more stones from the nearby paddocks, made mud from creek water poured onto freshly-dug dirt. The dirt was rock hard, but would he help? *Get a bloody move on.*

By the end of the week they had most of a chimney, chest-high walls, a gap for the new window, and blisters. By late autumn a hut with a roof, a chimney, a dusty window and a plank door hanging to the frame on leather hinges. The scrap man, his wife and Big Girl moved in. You was envious, but the next morning Wife informed her that the wind and flies droned through the hut; she was better off sleeping under the wagon.

Day by day the sky changed, the clouds always massing over the plain, the air cooler and the days shorter. It was time to take to the road again. But they had yet to buy a stronger horse and had nowhere near enough goods to sell.

•

ONE AFTERNOON THE air crackled, felt electrically strange and began to rumble and mutter. By evening they could see great, vivid lightning forks and sheets and snaking tongues in the east. You whimpered. She crawled under the wagon and planted her hands over her eyes, rocking inconsolably. *She had failed to look away. She had laid eyes on the storm*. She knew what that meant: her face would be stuck in a fearful grimace, the face she'd worn when the first lightning flash tricked her.

In the morning, the others still asleep, she crawled out and walked unsteadily to her trap line. Reached the creek bank – and halted, stunned. Such devastation she'd never seen before. Stormwater had barrelled down during the night, tumbling dead sheep, fencing wire, rabbit traps, twigs, branches, a bicycle wheel, a zinc bucket and scraps of wood, fabric and metal in configurations that no soul could ever disentangle or name. Otherwise, there was water, no longer storming through but still pouring from one shallow depression to the next. With the sun out, every pool was full of the sky.

'Flash flood,' said Wife behind her.

You, startled, clamped both hands over her face, mutely imploring: *Don't look, my face is stuck in storm fright*.

But Wife said nothing. In this family, a hand held to face, ribs, stomach, upper arm or anywhere at all was a sign of injury and pain. No one dared query or comment lest the scrap man feel he'd been judged. In this family, misery was a private concern.

Instead, Wife said, 'Gettin' a horse t'day,' and wandered back to the hut.

A horse. You perked up. I will teach him the way to the traps and back to his pen, she thought. I will show him to his water trough and tray of oats.

Something gleamed up at her from the storm-wracked creek bed, where tumbled stones lay washed clean by the flood. She slipped and slithered at an angle across the sloping bank and crouched over her find. Two finds: a knobbly lump of gold the size of her little toe and a doll's house cradle with a cracked rocker. Both sat in a puddle as if waiting for her. She leaned in, her nose almost touching the water, and saw, as if in a mirror, her face as it had always been. She could scarcely breathe. She was whole and unaltered and had found treasures. This was the best day of her life. Except her flour-bag dress didn't have pockets.

•

THE SCRAP MAN'S voice sounded behind her: 'Get off your backside and give me a hand.'

Still crouched, still examining her flawless face, You popped the nugget into her mouth and closed her fist around the cradle. Only then did she stand and face him.

He scrambled down to her and gestured both ways along the creek. 'Grab anything we can use. Wire, tins, boxes. Manna from heaven. I even saw a wheel off a bike. Whatcha got there?'

Frowning as he said it, his explosive eyebrows bunching, his fingers unbending hers. 'Rubbish,' he said, and threw the cradle into the deepest pool. 'Go on, get to work.'

With the imprint of his toecap on her behind, You spent the morning sloshing up and down the creek, pulling out rope, wire, planks, a pressed-tin ceiling panel – however did that end up in the creek? – and the bicycle wheel. Her fingers, palms, feet and legs dripped blood. She almost swallowed the nugget more than once. She didn't spot any more nuggets.

•

WHEN IT WAS midday by her reckoning, the sun at its highest point, You returned to the camp. No sign of Big Girl but Wife and the scrap man were at the pen, where a stranger sat astride a horse. He was leading a second horse, a graceful big brown, on a lead. Thinking he was the Education, You hid, ducking into the gap where the chimney protruded from the wall of the hut.

She waited. She could hear Big Girl inside, also hiding – Big Girl who was so big now, and given to effortful grunts as she waited for her baby to come. Darting a look around the edge of the chimney, You saw the stranger dismount and apparently glance her way. She jerked back, making herself as skinny as possible.

And that was when she saw, among all the chimney stones she'd been forced to carry and poke into position, a stone with a dimpled cavity shaped like a comma on its side. She took the nugget from her mouth, thumbed it tightly into the hole. Then, checking that the adults' backs were turned, she scooped up a dollop of mud and sealed her treasure in place. With the afternoon sun drenching the chimney wall, the mud plug would soon dry and be hard to spot.

But would she ever find it again if weeks and months and years went by? She couldn't read or write or reckon numbers, couldn't come back next year and count one, two, three, four, five stones up from the bottom and two from the right. She didn't know left and right, just one side or the other.

You knew the shape of a wedge-tail in the sky, however. The sound of an echidna burrowing towards invisibility in a mess of fallen leaves. The colour of lamplight and the smell of a stinkbug and the taste of honey in the pretty blue flowers of Paterson's curse. So it was an easy matter to dream her way into, and remember, the stone with the plugged hollow. She began to see, on its eroded, pitted and messy surface, a likeness of the old nag when he twisted his head around to seek her with his big, frightened, trusting eyes. One blink and the image was gone. Another and he was there again. She was satisfied. She didn't need to count numbers to memorise her hiding place: sight, smell and touch were just as good.

And why did the nugget matter? Way back in a corner of her mind was a thought she was almost too frightened to shine a light on: *One day she would run away.*

The scrap man was hollering, 'You. Get your arse here.'

She stepped casually from the chimney niche and crossed the yard to the pen, where the scrap man was talking money.

'You sure he's a two-year-old?'

'Positive,' said the man selling the horse.

'Strong?' muttered the scrap man doubtfully.

'A good Irish Draught, won't let you down,' the man said.

You stole a look at the stranger. He wasn't the Education or the Social but a flinty, resolute, narrow-faced man. He didn't look the type to let the scrap man beat him down in price. Wife seemed to know that, too, and together the womenfolk watched the scrap man waste his breath for twenty minutes.

The horse's age. How many hands high he was. Did he need reshoeing? The condition of his teeth. Did he have gas? Had he been beaten? You and Wife thought: That's a laugh, from the king of horse beaters.

The seller grew bored with the scrap man. He cast a sly gaze over You and said from the corner of his mouth: 'The kid, she a good worker?'

You felt her heart jump. She had a strange memory of many sisters, a house in a clearing, her father and money changing hands.

She swallowed, looked uneasily at the scrap man. He glanced at her vaguely, then at the horse . . . and a light went on in his head. You saw him think it through: Throw in the kid, pay less for the horse. Fewer mouths to feed – but fewer hands to work the traps, make goods to sell, help him on the open road. Big Girl, heavily pregnant, was temporarily useless to him. Wife had always been a disappointment.

He finally drew on his cigarette, jetted smoke to one side and said, 'Can't do it, mate.'

'The price stands,' the stranger said, forgetting You. Indicating the horse, he said, 'That there is a damn good Irish.'

'Lot of money.'

Wife stepped in. 'We got it.'

The scrap man looked at her, astounded. 'What do you mean?'

'From the skins and that,' she said, putting a protective arm across her face.

The scrap man, furious, caught a cold look in the stranger's face – *the type of cove to bash his wife* – and muttered, 'Very well, we'll take it.'

•

LUNCH WAS PIGEON stew, You slurping flecks of watery meat and carrots from a tin mug. She sat in a chilly wind, her back to a wheel of the wagon, while over by the fire the scrap man downed sherry and fed his rage. All that money on a bloody horse. And how long had Wife been putting so much money aside? Devious, that's what that was. It was *his* money. Was she a whore? Had she been selling herself? As for Big Girl, she was useless, a bloody great lump. He stormed, voice, fists, boots, the flat of his hand: Did they all think he was made of money? Now look what you made me do. Get up. Stop your snivelling.

You tried to tune out the thuds and the cries. He would watch Wife like a hawk now. He would think they were all keeping things from him. Meanwhile, it wasn't as if he'd bought a clapped-out wreck ready for the glue factory: the new horse was a beauty, a powerful big fellow with flesh on his bones and a glossy hide.

Eating quickly, she left before he found fault with her, too, and wandered across the yard to the horse pen. The old horse snickered a welcome, the new was wild-eyed, snorting, stamping. A great shudder rippled along his flank as she slipped into the pen. But then, as she came closer – smiling, humming 'Sing a song of sixpence' – and placed her hand on his neck, he stopped trembling. He stood placidly, receiving her touch, seeking more.

'Good boy,' You murmured. 'Irish,' she said, testing the name on her tongue.

He was firm and warm and clean. She stroked his neck and leaned her cheek against his. She fetched hay for both horses, filled the water trough.

But there, in the distance, was the scrap man. He'd emerged from the tent with a stockwhip and was standing at rocky attention as if trying to recall what came next. Oh yes: show the new horse who's boss.

You ran to head him off.

•

'DON'T!'

The scrap man blinked. 'What?'

'Don't hurt him.'

'Why, you little –'

He knew how to use a whip. It snapped and whistled, the tip lashing her bare legs, her cheeks, her raised forearms. Meanwhile You dodged and weaved, keeping a tree, a tarpaulin shelter, between herself and the new horse. She didn't want Irish to bear witness. He would never settle if he did.

'Come here, you little –' roared the scrap man.

You back-pedalled, skipping out of reach of the whip. Suddenly the scrap man sat down in surprise. He wavered. He keeled over. A ripping snort and he started to snore. You stopped, breathing hard, her body on fire. She returned to

Irish, who was chewing contentedly, thank God. 'Sing a song of sixpence,' she sang, her hand against his long face.

•

THE NEXT DAY she could scarcely move.

Yet the scrap man's memory was a clean slate. 'Don't just stand there,' he said. 'Show this bloody nag the way the things are done around here.'

Take Irish along the trap line, she thought, get him used to pulling wagon, buggy and cart. She took a step back from the scrap man. He stank, his little eyes pink and moist.

He thrust his chin at her. 'We're leaving soon, understand? I need everyone to get off their arse.' Get off their arse and make money. Get off their arse and make goods to sell.

You entered the pen and sang to Irish, her little hands patting and stroking.

'He's your responsibility,' said the scrap man, wandering back to the campfire.

•

FOR TWO DAYS her body burned. Nothing she did was unconscious: every movement required thought, to lessen the pain. Neither Wife nor Big Girl would soothe her, even if they could: the scrap man was always near, all of his money gone on horse-buying, and if you were one of his females your position was simple: *Sooner you than me.*

Alone in her pain, You trained Irish, taking him around the traps and back again, hauling the wagon from one end of the stony acres to the next. And presently this bitter thought lodged in her head: You and me against him, you and me against them. She pictured a long, empty, beckoning road. There was a house full of her brothers and sisters at the other end, just out of view. She could feel Irish rippling under her, free as the wind, helping her flee.

•

SHE MADE HER escape before the others stirred.

Up at dawn, a spare calico dress and Wife's woollen coat stuffed into an empty sugar bag, riding Irish to the trap line in case anyone was looking. Then, as soon as she was out of view, she headed across the paddocks to the distant road. The horizon was misty, the air cool, but with the rising of the sun and the heat from Irish's long, muscular motions, she was soon comfortable. The road ran dead straight across the plain and all she saw were birds, a distant couple of trees and fresh green shoots where there had been dead grass for months. She passed farm gates, saw the distant rooftops behind lines of cypress trees, and thought she could trade the nugget for food.

She had forgotten the nugget.

At mid-morning she came to a town, one short street with four side streets running from it east and west. She had rarely seen a town before. She was always hidden away in the back of the wagon, beneath the canopy with Big Girl, whenever Wife and the scrap man made their long buying and selling treks through the back country. If they came to a town, the scrap man, Wife seated beside him, would snarl over his shoulder at the girls: 'Keep your bloody heads down, don't talk to no one.'

You paused now beside a rundown house at the edge of the town. A yappy dog raced at the fence, maddened to see her there, and soon a woman stepped out, shading her eyes. You clicked her tongue to get Irish going again. What if the woman spoke? What could she say back to her?

Another house, a shopfront under a broad veranda, a couple of buggies outside a red-brick, white-columned bank, then more houses and finally a school yard at the other end of the town. Children raced here and there and hopped on one foot from square to square. They chatted and they sat on swings. They chewed apples and bits of bread. But they stopped to see You there on a horse, a tiny shape on a vast brown shape. They gathered at the fence, all ages, and not in great numbers, but more children together in one place than You had ever seen before.

'Who're you?'

'You coming here?'

'What grade you in?'

'You're late, it's recess.'

'What's your name?'

What was her name? It was You. She watched them with-draw from the fence line then, called by a man wearing a suit and tie. He'd emerged from the one-roomed school building, tolling a handbell, and he shaded his eyes to see her there on the road. She moved on.

•

By mid-afternoon she was sore, hungry, thirsty, and so was Irish.

She came to no other town. She saw only the road, winding over foothills, leaving the plain behind, and distant farm-houses, grazing sheep, windbreak trees and haystacks. Once a truckload of hay overtook her, the old jalopy rumbling and popping with effort. Sometimes shapes swam in the road ahead, as if water lay there, but it was never water, only strange shimmers.

And then out of the shimmers came a white horse pulling a sulky, two kids aboard, a girl flicking the reins, a little boy beside her, their schoolbags at their feet. So there must be a town ahead, with a school, school over for the day. They eyed her warily and, before reaching her, turned off through an open gateway in a wire fence and down a rutted track leading to a green roof behind cypress trees.

When they had vanished, You dismounted and approached the gateway. It consisted of two squat gum-tree posts with a gate of bent pipe and rusted wire hinged to one of the posts. Nailed on its side to the second post was a kerosene tin with the end cut off, home to spiders and sometimes letters and parcels.

But You was mostly interested in identifying what manner of people lived in the house. She was hungry, thirsty, needed a bed for the night – but would she be made welcome? She needed a sign.

She examined one gatepost, then the other. She'd been well taught by the scrap man on their travels along the farm roads. A schemer, a plotter, a trickster, he needed to be able to read people, needed to shapeshift from honest tinker to loving husband and father to devout churchgoer to farmhand and back again. But first he would scout around to see if another man of the road had left a sign. A passing swagman who'd been offered a rock bun and a cuppa at a farmhouse might leave a pair of stones on top of an entryway gatepost. If he'd been warned off by shotgun, dogs or a boot up the arse, he might carve a cross in the post or tie a black thread to the bottom fence wire.

You found a pair of crossed slashes in the weathered wood of the second post. She rocked back on her heels, suddenly afraid. These people might do her harm. They might be more than miserable skinflints and liable to turn their dogs on her.

Crouched like that, looking fearfully down the track to the hidden house, she failed to notice the bull ant on her foot until the pain stabbed her. She jumped and kicked and ran around, possessed by pain. It was razor blades cutting her flesh, burning match heads pressed against her, needles stabbing in and out. Dizzying pain. What could she do but ride it out? It wouldn't ride out. She stood tremblingly still, fists balled, and took her mind to where beauty resided. The doll's house. The old horse looking back at her. Someone dimly long ago brushing her hair. The perfect little nugget of gold she'd left behind. Until eventually the pain ebbed to a bad memory.

She mounted Irish and another horse was there suddenly. The man from the Education in his fine boots and hat and white shirt.

'Someone said they'd seen you heading this way,' he said, beaming at her.

His delivery was slow, loud, precise, as if she were slow-witted. Well, that's what he'd been told.

'Do . . . you . . . remember . . . me?'

You was feeble-mindedly blank.

A slight frown as he looked at her, a closer look this time.

'Can you count to ten?'

You opened her mouth and let all expression and nous leave her face.

'Can you add one and one together?'

You stared blankly at the ground.

'Do you know your two times tables?'

Nothing.

He came closer. She wasn't afraid of him, exactly, but officialdom frightened her because it frightened the scrap man.

He leaned in and said in a loud, slow, kind voice, 'What . . . is . . . your . . . name?'

You concentrated on the doll's house, the old horse's moist eyes, the red buttons on Wife's best dress and her gold nugget. Flowers. There were times when Wife and the scrap man sent her into gardens at the dead of night to dig up flowers, which they would pot and water and sell to the isolated farm women who wanted some colour in their lives. Last spring You had crept into a prideful town hall garden and returned with scarlet and yellow flowers shaped like little trumpets. A poultry farmer's wife bought them the next day. She said, 'Oh, what pretty garland lilies.'

'Lily,' whispered You.

•

'I FOUND HER just this side of Marraweeney,' said the Education, leaning over his pommel to address Wife and the scrap man.

Who pantomimed relief and bewilderment and gratitude and love. 'Much obliged to you, sir,' the scrap man said. 'When I think what could of happened . . .'

'Yes,' echoed Wife.

The Education waved off the thanks. He'd been leading Irish by the reins, and offered them to the scrap man now.

The scrap man stepped forward, Irish snorted, his eyes wild. The scrap man stepped back. The only solution that Lily could see was to climb down from the saddle and take the reins herself.

The Education watched her do it. Turning to the scrap man with a questioning look, he said, 'Are you sure Lily's feeble-minded?'

Momentarily perplexed, the scrap man almost said, 'Who?' He recovered quickly, tut-tutting and shaking his head as if to say his whole life had been sacrificed to the care of his daughter. 'Positive.'

Beside him Wife spoke up: 'She's not right in the head.'

'We tried her on the readin' and writin' and that,' said the scrap man. 'Took her to the doctor. Weren't no good.'

The Education cast a last dubious look at Lily. 'Very well then,' he said, wheeling around on his horse and heading back along the access track.

They watched him go. They waited in case he came back. And all that time, knowing what came next, Lily shrank her body, took her mind far away from the stony acres and the scrap man.

•

HE WORKED ON her in silence, fists and boots, and when she was on the ground he screamed, 'If you run away again, I'll kill you. Hear me?'

Not very well, owing to the fizzing, snapping and buzzing in her head. And down there in the dirt, Lily felt cross-eyed, barely able to focus on his toecaps, inches from her nose. She hawked and spat and there was a bloody front tooth in the dirt.

'And what's this "Lily" business? Don't get notions, hear?'

The toecaps wandered off and suddenly Big Girl was there, helping Lily stand, brushing her down. But Wife – half furious, half afraid – shook her. 'Get us all into trouble,' she hissed.

The voice came from far away, as though muffled by a blanket. Lily coughed, clearing the phlegmy blood in her throat. Coughed again and spat and Wife said, 'Here,' and tugged her towards the coals, where water simmered all day long in a black kettle. Lily followed, a slow-motion shuffle, all of her movements contained, minute. At the fire, she eased herself to the ground and let the wife and the big girl tend to her with cloths dampened in kettle water and applied once some of the heat had ebbed.

'What was you thinkin'?' demanded Wife. 'Could of starved to death. Could of had your throat cut. Brought the gov'ment down on us.'

'Get *us* into trouble, not just you,' said Big Girl.

When they were satisfied that Lily wouldn't die, could walk, no broken bones, Wife said, 'That will do you. Now I want you to help with the sewin'.'

Lily glanced at the piles of white calico flour bags, hessian sugar bags and old, holed singlets. Big Girl had been stitching for days – aprons, petticoats, dresses, pillowslips and pot mitts – but there was more to do before they ventured out on yet another long selling, trading and scrounging trip.

And time's pressing on the scrap man, Lily thought. He'll be thinking what if the Education sends the Social out here? A constable? A priest? And all of his money gone on buying a horse.

Lily picked up a torn bedsheet and cut out a piece large enough to make a pillowcase. If she ran again he would kill her, but the threat wasn't enough to take away her dreams. She dreamed of the long roads stretching, of Irish taking her away. She dreamed of reaching her hands into a doll's house and adjusting the position of a wardrobe. She saw the gold nugget concealed in the chimney stone – the image shattering because at that moment Big Girl heaved to her feet and stared down in fright at the water puddling between her toes.

Her chest in and out like a bellows, she said, 'I did a wee.'

'Your waters broke,' Wife said, a little sadly.

on the road

THE BABY DELAYED THEIR DEPARTURE.

One week passed, two, the scrap man fuming or casting panicky looks at the approach track to the stony acres. The women ignored him, fussing around the tiny child. 'Is she my sister?' whispered Lily.

The question taxed Wife. Her face creased in worry. 'I don't know. Could be.'

How could Lily run now? Leave her sister behind?

The baby was peaceful, slept most of the night, latched on to Big Girl's breasts without a fuss, and one day smiled at Lily. When all of that became clear to the scrap man he said, 'Bugger it, you're fit to travel.'

Arranging for one of his drinking mates to make regular checks on the old horse, he supervised the wagon loading. Fencing-wire toasting forks, some of which came apart as soon as they were moved, roofing-iron spatulas, calico and hessian skirts and aprons, potted jams and chutneys. Their own straw mattresses and bundled belongings – work clothes and a greasy suit for the scrap man, stitched-together rags and a time-worn proper dress with pockets for each of the girls. A bag of oats for Irish.

By early afternoon, an icy wind blowing, the sun crossing the sky at a shallow angle, they were rolling towards the road. The scrap man and his wife shared the bench seat looking down along Irish's rippling back, and Lily, Big Girl and the baby rocked and swayed with the petticoats and jars and rattling metalwork, hidden from the world. Lily was fascinated by the baby. She asked to hold her. She rocked and hummed and patted the minute spine. She wanted to fit the tiny pink bawling mouth to her own nipples, bringing comfort.

A mostly peaceful baby, but babies cry and the scrap man hated the noise. 'Shut her up or I'll shut her up for you,' he'd scream, jerking on the reins.

And so Big Girl and Lily would pat and croon and sing lullabies they barely remembered.

Late in the afternoon they reached the town where Lily had watched schoolchildren called to class by a clanging handbell. Slowly along the main street clopped Irish, the wagon creaking behind him, only a timid woman and a man wearing a cheeky smile and an engagingly tilted hat visible to the townspeople. But the baby could be heard, a thin sad pitiful wail. A woman loading groceries into a buckboard turned to watch their passage along the street, concern on her face. Concern from an old man with a walking stick and a young mother pushing a pram. A man whisking shop-floor dust out onto the footpath leaned on his broom and narrowed his eyes. And then the town policeman appeared in the road ahead, riding a neat, ears-pricked brown horse.

Taking no chances, the scrap man promptly turned left down a side street, left and left again until they reached the beginning of the town, where he turned right. They were back at the hut by nightfall. There was hell to pay from the scrap man. It was all their fault, the womenfolk.

Subsiding at last, he pointed at Wife and Big Girl. 'You and you, stay here with the baby. You,' he went on, turning to Lily, 'you're comin' with me.'

•

THE NEXT MORNING, Wife whispered, 'Keep your knees together,' then boosted Lily from the cold ground to the wagon seat beside the scrap man. Lily did not understand the warning precisely, but warnings were wasted, for she already knew the scrap man through and through.

The wagon creaked away, heaving like a galleon on a high sea. Lily glanced back at the hut, where Wife stood with Big Girl and her baby, and waved, just once, seeing a wave in return. She faced forward again and they retraced yesterday's route but with a detour around that town, and the days and weeks unfolded into winter and shorter daylight hours and erratic fortunes. The scrap man would sell a spatula, a pot of chutney or rabbit-fur mittens, plug a housewife's leaky kettle, buy horseshoes at a penny each and sell them for a penny ha'penny, but then fritter his earnings on a hand of cards, tobacco, a woman or sweet sherry, sometimes leaving Lily alone for a day and a night. At first he would chain her ankle to an eyebolt in the wagon floor, but eventually stopped the practice, as though it were burdensome or one too many things to remember. He'd warn her, 'Escape and I'll hunt you down, your life won't be worth living.'

That was the threat that mattered. Lily knew Wife and Big Girl were no match for him. Shivering under the piled rugs in the wagon or an abandoned barn, she'd visit her baby sister in her mind's eye. She'd visit the doll's house and move the rocking chair. She'd visit the nugget gleaming in its dark niche.

•

No LONGER HIDDEN from view, Lily became the scrap man's main asset. He quickly saw how the mugs took pity on this motherless, feeble-minded child in her thin best dress and hair in grimy yellow ribbons. Pleased with the sale of a toasting fork or table napkin at some farmhouse, he might impart one of his trickster's lessons to her. 'You need to know how to read someone,' he might say, flicking the reins as they trundled away.

Lily would have a silent laugh. She knew all of his crooked ways, and she'd been reading him forever. Reading the mugs, too, seeing their pity. And distaste, as if her feeble-mindedness were catching. When that happened the mugs were just as likely to turn the scrap man away as buy from him, but he wasn't canny enough to see it.

Another of his tricks was thievery, perfected on their previous journeys. A farmer's wife alone while her husband ploughed his paddocks would be diverted in her doorway by Wife, Big Girl and Lily, giving the scrap man time to poke about in the sheds. A farmer pottering in his barn while his wife was out shopping would be drawn into conversation by Wife and the scrap man, as the girls raided the house, Lily keeping watch, Big Girl slipping through doors and windows.

But last trip, Big Girl's belly got in the way, so they swapped roles, Lily with her light fingers, Big Girl on the lookout.

Their first opportunity this time came when a farmer told them he was too busy to buy anything and the wife was out with the kids, at a school picnic.

A stillness settled in the scrap man, an alertness. He began to fine-tune his dealings with the man. 'I buy scrap metal,' he offered.

The farmer removed his hat to think. A tidemark of grease ringed the hatband. His dome, balding, was mottled and pinkish under strands of hair combed back from a stark white forehead. The rest of him was sun-darkened and work-stained. Worn leather braces held his gaping pants at chest height.

He was unlovely. Lily looked away, towards the house. It was a low, sombre brick building surrounded by a cypress hedge. Flat paddocks behind it, stretching to the horizon, recently shot with little green spears of wheat or oats or barley. Already she was mapping her route through the hedge to the veranda and the best door or window.

'Any old iron droppers. Horseshoes.'

The farmer said, 'Got a couple of anvils you can have.'

He'd already turned from them and was crossing to the barn. The scrap man, climbing down from the wagon to follow, murmured to Lily, 'You know what to do.'

He paused. 'And no running off. We got a baby I can train up, remember.'

•

As soon as the men had disappeared into the barn, she raced across the yard and through the hedge. Down a side path to the back door. It was unlocked, so no need to wriggle through a window. Expecting noisy hinges, she inched open the door. It moved silently. She was in.

All houses had their inside smell. Lily identified perfume, bacon, cigarette smoke, the pine cones and dry eucalyptus leaves in a box beside the open hearth, where a fire had burned down to ash, furniture wax and people smells. She should rush, not linger, but a girl lived here, in a pretty room, and Lily burned to know her life.

There was a doll's house. She repositioned the piano. There were dolls with pink cheeks, books with gold-leaf writing, dresses on hangers.

A boy lived here. He owned lead soldiers and a cricket bat.

The furniture was dark and massive. There was a black piano with yellowed keys. She pressed one. The sound was flat and unmusical, but what did she know? She knew it didn't sound pure.

There were photographs on the sitting room wall of an old man standing behind a seated woman, a hand on her shoulder, and of a younger man on a horse. These men wore moustaches and the woman was buttoned to the throat.

Lily pocketed a shilling, two sixpences and a penny from a kitchen drawer. She didn't know how to count or add or read or write or buy goods in a shop, but she did know that the silvery coins were more desirable than the penny, even though smaller and lighter. She liked the silveriness. She added to the coins a hairclip from a mass of them in the girl's room, soap wrapped in pink tissue paper and a scarf from a tangle of them on a hook among hallway coats and hats.

She was back at the wagon with most of her goods stowed before the scrap man and the farmer returned, each man staggering under the weight of an anvil. She thought: Why carry them from barn to wagon when you could have driven the wagon to the barn?

The farmer saw this on her face, a fleeting intelligence, and frowned, so Lily went vacant again, eyes dull and mouth open, as if no sense had ever lurked inside her.

•

'How DID YOU do?' said the scrap man later.

Lily gave him the penny and the shilling. Anything less and there would have been hell to pay.

He seemed happy enough, having paid sixpence for the anvils. 'My best little housebreaker and pickpocket,' he said, giving her a wink, his way of expressing any kind of approval.

Needing to put miles between them and the farmer, he jiggled the reins at Irish to get a move on.

The hooves sounded through the hours. Lily dreamed. The sixpences were in the tea caddy, one place he'd never look, for he'd never had to brew tea with so many womenfolk to do it. The sixpences joined the pennies and ha'pennies she'd started gathering over the weeks, when it became clear the scrap man liked slow horses and fast women and the last drop in every bottle. Wife had warned her it might happen.

The scrap man had been musing on things, too. He said, out of nowhere, 'One day *you* are gonna be too big for climbin' through winders.'

The words took a moment to sink in. Lily huddled her shoulders in misery. So it hadn't been an idle threat, his saying he'd train Big Girl's baby in thievery when she was old enough. Lily brooded. Self-pity and a curious kind of jealousy shot through her to think she'd be replaced. She wanted to be the scrap man's best thief and pickpocket. And yet she didn't want to be valued in that way, didn't want the little one to be valued in that way.

•

LATE IN THE afternoon they came to a cottage on the edge of a town that nestled in a hollow between seven hills. Lily remembered the house from two years ago and tried to tell the scrap man to drive on, but he hated to be told anything. She sat mutely while he ran through his greeting to the woman who had come to her garden gate.

'Missus,' he said, with a gallant raising of his hat.

He didn't know it but his rakish charm was undone by his hair. It looked as if it had been combed with an angry cat. The woman stared at it in fascination. 'What do you want?'

'Top prices for your rags and scrap metal. Household repairs. Or would a fine lady such as yourself be interested in a pot of jam?'

'You sold me a toasting fork a couple of years ago.'

'Did I?' said the scrap man uneasily. 'In that case, could I interest you in –'

'It broke the first time I used it.'

'Oh, dear. Well, I –'

The woman gave him a humourless smile. 'I want my money back.'

The scrap man tutted in regret. 'Missus, my goods are made with the greatest care and finest craftsmanship you'll find outside Melbourne.'

The woman snorted.

'However, like with anything, if mistreated they won't work proper. But I tell you what I'm going to do for you today, I'm going to give you a discount on everything I have for sale, what do you say to that?'

'I'd say you were a thief. And answer me this: Did I mistreat my toasting fork when I placed a slice of bread on it? For that's all it took for the blessed thing to break.'

The woman was having great fun. Lily could see the gleam in her eye.

The scrap man had met his match. 'I'm afraid I must bid you goodbye, missus,' he said, trying for dignity but darting his gaze about for constables. He clicked his tongue at Irish.

Irish pulled, the wagon jerked into motion, and the woman shouted, 'How old is that girl? Six? Seven? She should be in school.'

•

THEY PUT MANY miles between themselves and that town, not stopping until the night was inky black. While Irish chewed on the meagre grass and drained a roadside puddle, Lily gathered pine cones, twigs and branches, and the scrap man lit a fire within a half-circle of paddock stones. The fire when it settled was smoky and weak, for the wood was damp. It barely warmed the kettle or melted the dripping in the frying pan – not that there was much to cook, only a pair of greenish mutton chops. Lily was often hungry these days, and if the scrap man had beer or sherry he wasn't interested in buying food.

That night he drank until the fire was dead, and Lily, pulling on both of her dresses, wrapping the stolen scarf three times around her throat and huddling under a couple of thin blankets, lay in the tray of the wagon. At one point in the frozen night the scrap man flopped beside her. His snores were like cotton sheets torn over and over again and the air was heavy with his beer farts.

•

IN THE MORNING Lily drove while he slept. Along main roads and back roads and occasionally down avenues of pine trees to houses behind tall hedges, where a woman might buy an oven mitt or a jar of chutney. Lily did not offer to buy anything, not when they were so poor. She'd say, when asked, 'My dad's not feeling well today.'

They'd glance doubtfully at the sounds of snoring. 'Why aren't you in school?'

'I'm starting at my new school next week,' Lily would say. 'We've only just moved to the area.'

•

SOON COLDER WINDS blew, bringing rain, bringing unfriendliness to every door they knocked on.

When Lily and the scrap man were low on hope, cash and food, they came to a town that supported three pubs, three churches, two primary schools, a high school, several shops, many houses and a railway line. Riding the wagon through from east to west and then from north to south, the scrap man said, 'I remember this place.'

Does it remember you? Lily wondered.

'Did quite well here. Years ago, it was. There's a flour mill.'

He took them to the mill, a disused bluestone building on a river outside of the town. It was foursquare and grim in the landscape, its glassless windows staring at Lily. Glassless meant empty, but this wasn't an empty place. Even when she was inside it, looking at the denuded rooms and hearing only the hollow boom of her footsteps on the wooden floor, Lily felt eyes at her back. The people of all the years of the building's existence were watching from dark corners.

She kept close to the scrap man.

He took her through to the wall beside the river waters and showed her the waterwheel and the sluice. He chatted away, but Lily was interested only in the signs of habitation: dead coals in an iron bucket, where people had cooked or warmed their hands; scraps of newspaper, some streaked with poo; beer bottles and cigarette butts; a hat. And a boot that, with its sole adrift, reminded her of a mouth in pain.

'Put your mattress there,' the scrap man said, pointing. 'Get a fire going.'

He began brushing road grime from his trousers, scraping the mud from his boots, shrugging his way into his best jacket and finger-combing his hair. 'Keep an eye on our things. Be back shortly.'

Lily knew the meaning of that. He'd walk into a pub with his cocky charm and be away for hours. She watched him ride Irish towards the town, leaving the wagon parked hard against an outside wall. Watch their things? How could she do that if she were asleep in the mill? She resolved to continue sleeping in the wagon, amid the pots and pans and folded clothes and mould-spotted jam.

On a sudden, panicky thought, Lily checked the tea caddy.

He'd found her stash of coins. Her mouth went dry, her heart thumped in her chest. Money to see the family through lean times, and he'll spend it all on beer, women and poker games. And he'll find a way to lay the blame at my feet.

Scrounging a few armfuls of twigs, boards and dry branches, Lily lit a fire in the centre of the mill's vast main room. She dozed, watching the flame shapes. Warmth. Light to drive the ghosts away.

•

LILY ATE NOTHING, for there was nothing to eat. Darkness fell and she huddled beside the fire until the coal eyes winked out, then left the building to crawl into the back of the wagon. She pulled every scrap of fabric over her little frame.

In the morning she headed down to the river and scooped water over her face and hands. Washed and awake and hungry, she walked to the town along a muddy road that serviced the farms further out along the river. As she walked, she gauged the time it took. She didn't know how to read a clock but measured time by the tasks that ordered her life. The walk to town took about as much time as a run of her rabbit traps.

Entering by the main street, she walked up and down and around and about and found Irish tied to a rail behind the meanest pub. His head hung dispiritedly, but as soon as he heard and smelled her his ears went up, he stamped his fore hoof and whinnied.

'Irish,' she whispered, stroking his neck.

The pub was shut tight. The scrap man could be anywhere in creation. Lily heard Wife's voice in her head: 'The bugger comes home stinking of his cheap tarts.'

Where in creation did a tart live? And he hadn't even removed the saddle; a wonder it hadn't been stolen overnight.

Fed up, Lily mounted Irish. She took him back to the river, which he tried to drain before snatching at all of the nearby grass with his giant teeth.

•

LATER ON SHE retraced her steps, intent on finding the scrap man. Passing a farmhouse on the outer edge of the town, she saw a rattletrap truck emerge from the driveway, a family on board, mother, father and two boys. They were dressed in their finest clothes and glanced in a superior way at Lily as they puttered by, disappearing down a street where church bells sounded with icy clarity in the wintry air.

Alone now, unobserved, Lily rode Irish along the farm driveway and around to sheds behind the house. Here was a haystack. Finding an empty wheat bag, she stuffed it with hay for later and gave another armful to Irish. He ate with a great, wet chomping of his teeth, the best feed he'd had in weeks.

Heading back to the mill, Lily took a short cut through the town. She reached a church and paused. People were emerging, shrugging into coats and shaking the minister's hand. Children streamed from a small, attached building, still looking brushed, combed and buttoned-up but mad to get out into the wildness of the air. Lily watched them play. They watched her, even as they raced around. She wanted to race with them, her arms out like wings.

Two kids came to the picket fence to stare at her.

'You stink.'

Lily swallowed. She gently flicked the reins and let Irish take her to safety. A pat of mud sailed past her shoulder and splattered against Irish's neck. He shied. She crooned to him and then they were out of range, on a broad street where the shops and banks squatted, waiting for Monday.

She swivel-necked as she rode by, peering at a dress on a dummy, a stack of soup tins, a barber's chair, a row of shiny boots and a shop where watering cans hung from ceiling hooks and ladders leaned against the walls. Last year the scrap man had sent her into such a place, saying he wanted her to buy him a tin of striped paint and a left-handed hammer. The customer standing next to her had howled with laughter, but the shopkeeper, seeing Lily's confusion, said tiredly, 'There are no such things, lass. Someone's pulling your leg.' Lily stomped out, burning with shame, ignored the scrap man when she clambered back onto the wagon. 'Don't tell me they've run out of paint and hammers,' he'd said.

Lily tried to shake off the memory. Memories did you no good at all.

•

BACK AT THE bluestone mill, she stowed the hay and sat and thought.

One of the scrap man's many rules of trickery and thieving was: 'You can't make a mug of anyone on a Sunday.'

Decent people don't want a rag-and-bone man turning up on their doorsteps on a Sunday, offering to sell them a pillowslip made from a threadbare sheet, buy their scrap metal, fix their sticking kitchen drawers. 'Their heads are full of churchgoin',' the scrap man explained. 'All that preachin' turns them nasty and mean.'

But Lily had no money, no food. She didn't know when the scrap man would find his way back to her, but she did know he'd be hungry, broke and foul-tempered.

On the other hand, money was no good to her today. The shops were shut.

But she was hungry.

She changed her dress, washed again at the river and worked the tangles from her hair with her nerveless cold fingers.

Back onto Irish.

•

SHE CHOSE A house where children lived, as revealed by a tricycle and a wooden fire engine on the veranda.

A man answered her knock, still wearing his church best, trousers, shirt, tie, waistcoat and shiny shoes. He glanced at

Irish, on the other side of his fence, then back at Lily, an impudent presence on his doorstep. 'Yes?'

'Hello, my name's Lily and me and my dad just arrived today and –'

'What do you want?'

He wasn't a man who worked with his hands. Soft, white, clean hands and a soft, white, clean, precise, mean, God-fearing face. Lily said, 'Er, which way to the station?'

Casting an irritated glance at Irish, he pointed left and shut the door in her face.

She walked Irish to the next street, where she found a rambling house. A house is like a person, she thought. Some let you in and others shut you out. This one had a treehouse and a sandpit in the back yard and whoever lived there was not particularly fussy about weeds or hedge neatness.

The mother answered Lily's knock. She was full of smiles and motherliness to see her there. 'Hello, dear.'

'Hello, my name's Lily and me and my dad just arrived today for his new job but all our food's on the buggy, which broke an axle on the way here and I was wondering if you could spare some eggs and milk and bread, thank you very much.'

It was her longest sentence ever, and she was astonished she'd made it through to the end. She watched the woman sort through it, her face reflecting her thoughts: concern, a touch of suspicion, the need to give comfort.

'Where is your dad?'

'Getting the keys to our new house.'

'Where?'

'Over by the dump.'

'So you'll be starting school here?'

'Yes, lady.'

'What work does your father do?'

He gets his slaves to make money for him, then drinks it all away, thought Lily.

'He's got a job on the railway,' she said.

Standing there, she was frozen through, skin blotchy and teeth juddering, and the woman said, 'You poor little mite, come inside and get warm.'

Lily had never been inside a house that lived and breathed with people, only houses abandoned for the day. This house was full of light, cooking smells and shimmering heat. A man and two children sat at the kitchen table, still brushed and combed from church, but they'd changed into neat weekend pants, skirts and pullovers. The man smiled, lifting an eyebrow at his wife. The children were utterly still, staring avidly at Lily, but she didn't see mud-throwing in their natures.

'This is Lily. She's new, and in a bit of bother.'

The mother explained what the bother was and the father said, 'Of course we can help,' and Lily left the house with a small wooden crate containing cow's milk in a billycan, four eggs wrapped in tissue paper, two apples, a carrot and sliced meat, still warm from the Sunday roast.

The mother, handing her the crate when Lily was safely mounted on Irish, said, 'Careful you don't tip.'

'Thank you.'

'Bring back the billy and the box when you can, no hurry.'

'Thank you.'

She'd hide them in the meantime, for both were worth money to the scrap man. 'Cheerio.'

'Cheerio, dear.'

Concealing the crate and the billy in one of the mill's waterwheel buckets, Lily rode back and found another welcoming house, and another. By late afternoon she had sufficient food for a week and returned bum-sore from all of that riding up and down the length of the town with her hand out.

•

SHE NO LONGER had the mill to herself.

Two swaggies had installed themselves in her absence. They'd piled her precious firewood on the morning's coals and were sprawled beside the flames, surrounded by empty bottles. Seeing Lily appear, they got unsteadily to their feet and roared a greeting as if she were a long-lost friend.

'Have a drink, girlie!'

'Come and give us a kiss!'

Lily took a step back. Despite the fact that one man had a bent nose, the other a lazy eye, they were alike: bleary, unshaven, their boots held together with fencing wire, their clothing ripped and stained. And despite the fire's heat, they gave off a greasy dankness. Retreating, she raced to the wagon, poked her head in. Everything was intact, but give them time . . .

'Come on, love!' they called. 'Have a drink with us. Plenty for everyone.'

Lily returned to the fire. 'No,' she said firmly.

'Ah,' said crooked nose in disgust, 'more for us, then.'

They collapsed beside the fire again. Darkness crept in and they grew raucous, roaring songs, arguing, weeping, confessing to old sins and heartbreaks. They argued – with each other, with demons Lily couldn't see. They would stand and swing punches at each other, wrestle, collapse again.

Frightened, Lily settled herself in the chilly wagon, ate beans cold from a tin, wondered what to do if the scrap man failed to return. He had all their money. By now he would have *lost* all their money. Tomorrow she would take the wagon door to door, she had no other choice.

Eventually the swagmen fell silent. Lily climbed down, tiptoed to the mill door, looked in. They were asleep beside the coals, lazy eye so close his pants were about to singe. With an icky feeling, she grasped his greasy shoulder and rolled him clear.

But in the cold dark of midnight, the wagon tilted. A hand groped beneath her bedding. She gagged, such a pissy, poo-streaked, oily, crusty stench on the man trying to climb aboard. It was crooked nose, and Lily conked him with the frying pan. He shrank away. She didn't sleep. And in the morning he was simply snoring beside the fire with his mate, a knob on his forehead.

•

STILL NO SCRAP man.

Hitching Irish to the wagon, Lily drove into town and began selling door-to-door. It was a place of long, broad streets and leafy cross streets; you'd take days to see it all at horse-and-wagon pace, but she had a clear sense of where she had been yesterday and where she should go next, in her methodical quartering of the town from one end to the other.

She did not call at every house, in some streets she did not stop at all, for she was seeking warm houses. Warmth to Lily was the presence of chimney smoke, toys, a pleasant woman pottering in her front yard, a little panting, tail-whipping dog full of joy to see her there outside the gate. Houses and people were warm if warm lights and colours rose around them. The scrap man, by contrast, gave off a chilly wind.

Her approach, with some variation, was to say that she was the motherless child of a father who needed to see a city doctor next week and they were saving for the train fare. Or the child of an abandoned mother pausing in the town on her way to her people down south, we must start all over again, can you help? Or she was newly arrived in the town and starting at the primary school next week and Mum and Dad were spending the day fixing the new house.

Some said to her, 'Are youse gypsies?'

Lily didn't know whether or not she was a gypsy, only that gypsies were loathed and feared. 'No.'

'Whatcha sellin' again?'

Jams, chutneys, pillowslips, oven mitts, toasting forks, one remaining spatula, one block of fine soap wrapped in tissue paper that she said her dead mother had left her, and sundry dresses and petticoats.

'Are youse buyin'?'

Not at first. She wanted money coming in, not going out. But by lunchtime, a few ha'pennies, pennies, and threepenny and sixpenny bits in her possession, Lily did start buying in tiny amounts. She would flick her expert gaze over the rags and scrap metal and quote a measly price – just like the scrap man. Her fierce canniness amused people. Most of them accepted with a grin and a head shake.

The wagon full of junk by mid-afternoon, she returned to the mill. Crooked nose and lazy eye were staring dully at the dead coals; they barely registered her. Keeping her distance, watching for sudden movements, she rebuilt the fire and climbed into the wagon to sort through her takings. The rags she would keep for the summer months of sewing and stitching with Wife and Big Girl back at the hut. The scrap metal she would sell tomorrow to the scrap dealer who had a yard beside the railway station. Name her price, her jaw out stubbornly, so he would know she could not be cheated by anyone.

She began to sift through the rags, her quick, assessing fingers testing seams and tensile strength. And there at the centre of one bundle was a tight red ball.

A dress.

It seemed to sigh in relief as she shook it, to fill with air, shimmer and dance. It was corduroy, thick, warm. It had never been repaired or even needed repair. The red was the redness of a dark red rose. Mine, thought Lily. She had never owned a dress that was not once a grain sack.

It fit her perfectly, close but not too close around her torso, long and comforting in the sleeves and down over her knees. The skirt was pleated. It swirled when she spun around on her toes. There were loops for a belt but she lacked a belt, which didn't matter for she was bound to be sold or given a belt one day. It smelled of soap, not an unknown girl's body.

•

LILY'S FINAL CHORE: return the kind lady's billy and wooden crate.

She wore the dress. It would be proof to the lady and to everyone who might stop her that she was not a vagrant girl but settling in nicely here.

And the first thing the lady said was, 'What a lovely dress.'

Then she said, 'The children have just come home from school. Have you time for a play?'

Lily swallowed. She looked around at Irish, tied to the gate; Irish looked at her. She turned back to the woman and whispered, 'Yes.'

She had never played before. She had never spent time with children before.

The woman took her through the freshly baked bread– smelling house to a large sunroom at the back, where there was some sun, coming in low and wintry over next door's hedge. The children were on the floor, the girl seated on her heels and attending in a fussy, absorbed way to her dolls and their dresses, the boy to lead soldiers and cannon on the battlefield slopes and ravines of a tartan blanket. He made gun noises.

'Children, you remember Lily? Lily, this is Thelma and this is Noel.'

Then Lily was alone with them and they stared. Time stopped. Nothing happened. Finally Thelma thrust a doll at Lily and Noel positioned an infantryman behind a blanket fold and Lily steeled herself to crouch and ape the movements of the girl. Remove the dress from the doll, try another. Help it to walk and dance. Fluff up the hair. Thelma was quite incurious, as though Lily were here every day. Curiosity burned in Lily but she hadn't the language to express it, and after one hour the lady was there, saying, 'I'm sure Lily's father is wondering where she is.'

Lily thought: I'm wondering where *he* is. She got to her feet.

'Thelma, perhaps Lily would like to take Rosalind home with her.'

Rosalind was a doll with floppy limbs and a hard cracked face with fading painted eyebrows and rosebud lips and skull holes where the hair was coming out, but beautiful to Lily. As beautiful as the doll's house back home and the gold nugget and Big Girl's baby.

'Mine to keep?' whispered Lily. To hide from the scrap man, who would sell her for tuppence, quick as a flash.

'Yes, dear. Thelma doesn't play with her anymore, do you, sweetheart?'

For just a moment there was a faint dark corona around Thelma's head, until she mustered her goodness and smiled at Lily and proffered the doll. 'Here.'

Lily whispered thank you and floated out to Irish and through the streets to the river and the mill. The floaty feeling left her once or twice, though. She had a sensation of eyes watching from behind. She pulled on the reins, stopped and peered back the way she'd come, and saw nothing, but felt certain eyes were watching how she went, and where.

•

THE NEXT MORNING, Lily took the iron bolts, brass candle-sticks and copper tubing to the scrap dealer. His name was Morrison, and he had a round unlined face like a scary baby. He wasn't interested in haggling. Quoting a low price, he wouldn't budge, and Lily knew she had no choice but to accept.

She returned to her door-to-door selling with a vengeance, and by the afternoon had amassed a noisy collection of coins, which she stowed in an unsold oven mitt. One woman, watching Lily drop a sixpence into the mitt, said, 'That's not going to last the distance, dear.'

Lily eyed the mitt. It was lumpy, threadbare and stretched at the seams.

'You're in danger of spilling everything,' the woman continued. 'Take my advice, get the bank to exchange it for paper money.'

Lily tried to ignore the advice. But the mitt was heavy, straining. And then a threepence slipped through a gap in the stitching and rolled into the gutter, so Lily went clinking into the bank.

'Paper money, please.'

The teller, a man in trousers, a tie, a waistcoat and a vivid white shirt, metal bands around the sleeves, looked down his nose and over the counter at her. He was perfectly clean, even his nails. Clean, moist pink tongue and one tooth a little skewed. She couldn't look at his eyes.

'Why aren't you at school, young lady?'

One of Lily's well-rehearsed explanations flowed across the dully gleaming wooden counter, to which the teller shook his head doubtfully. 'Aren't you the little girl who's been driving a horse and cart door to door?'

Lily went very still. She began to shepherd the coins back across the counter to the mouth of the oven mitt.

The teller stopped her. 'Now, now, I'm not going to tell anyone. You shall have your banknotes.'

Using the edge of his hand, he drew the coins towards him and sorted them into piles: sixpenny bits, threepenny bits, pennies, ha'pennies, several shilling pieces and five chunky florins. His lips moved as he counted, belying his fingers, which blurred in movement. Then he was counting out the paper money, a few ten-shilling notes.

'Easier to carry?' he guessed.

Easier to hide from the scrap man, Lily thought. 'Yes.'

But there were coins left over. 'Eight shillings and three-pence ha'penny,' the teller said. 'Not quite enough for another note,' he added, seeing Lily's confusion.

She burned inside: he knew that she could not count. She could not count, add, subtract, divide, spell or write. She knew the ants busy in the dirt, the habits of the birds in nesting season and the movements of the sun and the moon. She could anticipate the mood and intent of the scrap man. But none of that was sufficient here, and she scuttled away from the bank feeling obscurely cheated and wanting to burst.

•

BACK AT THE mill she could hear the swaggies muttering on the other side of the bluestone walls. Where to hide the money from nosy parkers? Not the tea caddy, nor any other container, for the scrap man would sniff it out.

Her gaze was drawn to the saddle seam, the frayed stitching. She dug around in the gap, widening it, and slipped in the paper money. Sealed it with a needle and thread. The eight shillings and threepence ha'penny went into the tea caddy, for the scrap man to find. To *appease* the scrap man, who might lose whole weeks of his life from time to time but would surely remember why he was on the road with Lily and demand to know where the money was, given that she'd sold so many things in his absence.

She sealed the tea caddy, climbed down from the wagon, and in the nick of time, too, for one of the muttering voices inside the mill had been the scrap man. Suddenly there he was, no apology or explanation or even hello.

'Where you been?' demanded Lily, feeling cross.

He looked at her, full of the sickly pale tremors of a man returned from a drinking binge. 'None of your business.'

Pushing by her, he boarded the wagon and started poking about, kicking at her neat piles of rags, rattling the box of toasting forks. He stuck his head out. 'You been sellin',' he said accusingly.

'Yes.'

He climbed down, she put her forearm across her face. But he didn't strike her.

'Good. Where's the money?'

'Usual place.'

He climbed aboard again, emptied eight shillings and threepence into his coat pocket, joined her on the ground.

'We need to take money home with us,' Lily said. 'We need to buy food.'

Again she shielded her face, but he'd already forgotten her, his blockish features blurred and vacant, as if sketched by a blunt crayon. He staggered into the mill. A cry went up, crooked nose and lazy eye greeting him like an old friend.

•

LILY WATCHED THEM from the shadows.

The scrap man was a best new chum to the others. He had money; he liked to play poker; and he played as he drank, lustily, carelessly.

An hour later, his pockets were empty, his bottle dry. This was the dangerous time. Lily got ready to intervene, starting forward as he threw down his cards, roared, 'You're a pair of thieving mongrels,' and launched himself at the swagmen.

Just then they all heard a pair of horses pull up outside. As silent as a wisp of smoke, Lily slipped out through a side window and crouched where she could hear and see. Two horses, two men, one a priest, the other one of those buttoned-down men who like to enter government service. She could see them standing in the main doorway to the mill, two shapes outlined against the weak sun. Then they were crossing the floor to the sad drunks, who had meanwhile regrouped like civilised creatures to sit innocently around the fire.

'Good afternoon,' the priest said.

The scrap man and the swagmen continued their charade, bent over their playing cards.

'I'm Father Kenny and this is Mr Reid from Social Services,' persisted the priest.

'Pleased to meet you,' the scrap man said presently. He didn't look up. He slapped down his cards. 'Two pairs.'

The Social cleared his throat. 'You have a little girl with you. We are concerned for her welfare.'

The scrap man flicked the ash off his cigarette and said, 'Don't know what you're talking about.'

'Come now,' the priest said. 'She has been going door to door with that very horse and wagon outside. She should be in school. Where is her mother?'

Mother? Lily tried to conjure her mother, but she was no longer sure of her memories of a woman standing with many children on a patch of dirt, the mallee scrub pressing in. They were not memories but wispy thoughts.

She clenched her fists. Pay attention, she told herself. It was possible she'd been followed by the Thelma and Noel mother. Someone had been watching her. This was a town where people watched and took note.

'We just got here,' the scrap man was saying now. 'As you can see, there's no kid. We got better things to do than listen to some God-botherer.'

'You three are travelling together?'

'What's it to you?'

'Where is the child? Have you harmed her?' said Reid.

Lily could tell from his voice and tilted-back head that the stink of the men was in his nostrils.

'Your turn to deal,' said the scrap man to the swaggie with the dented skull.

The Social and the priest gave up after a while. They walked out into the grey light and mounted their horses and Lily thought her days here with the scrap man were numbered, but try telling him that when he had the grog in him.

•

ALL THE NEXT day the men played poker, the scrap man winning and losing on epic scales if his voice and manner were any indication. At one point in the afternoon one of the swagmen staggered off with his winnings and returned with beer, which he shared with the others, for winning had put him in a good mood. Lily took herself to bed after sunset and the men continued to drink and gamble, and at dawn they were snoring and the fire was out. At noon they emerged, blinking, to piss and gather wood and go back to what they were doing, and Lily knew for sure there was no money left but the paper money folded into the saddle.

What could she do if they were almost out of goods to sell? She fossicked for gold, but this was a rushing kind of river and there were no stones or pebbles or pools visible where gold might lurk. She was known in the town so she could not sell the remaining goods. She fretted. It was time to move on.

She suggested this the next morning. The scrap man frowned, bewildered. 'We are flat, stony broke,' she told him.

His face cleared. 'You're right,' he said.

The next moment he was harnessing Irish to the wagon, dragging Lily aboard, creaking them away from the mill. Lily's burden lifted. Down along the river road they went, to the outlying farms, where they sold the last spatula, a billycan, a pillowslip and a couple of rabbit-fur mittens. It was like old times, the scrap man fresh and canny as if he'd never had a drink in his life. They amassed a few coins and were donated a few old shirts and sheets and invited to stay for tea and rock buns at a house that had a smooth round stone on the gatepost.

Yes, it was like old times, for as they left that house, the scrap man removed the stone and tossed it in the dense grass of the roadside ditch. He was the true devil. He would stake an advantage over everybody, even to denying the next man of the road a cup of tea and a rock bun at that house. Lily hated him.

Hated him more when he turned the wagon around and drove them back to the bluestone mill. He jumped out and ran to the doorway, crying out in his nasty way, 'Now you bastards will see how the game is played.'

And so they stayed. He drank and gambled.

That evening Lily was in the wagon, not yet asleep but wool-gathering, Big Girl's baby in her mind's eye, when the scrap man and lazy eye came to her. They stared, measuring her with a cold gaze, her length, width and character, the scrap man saying, 'Two quid.'

'Two quid? You're dreaming. I'll give you a guinea for her.'

'Quid and a half.'

'One pound five.'

Lily said, 'I am not for sale,' and tumbled over the side and was on Irish and riding him away before they knew it.

But she had nowhere to sleep and the town had spies out for her, so she returned to the mill and hid in a musty corner until the men had drunk themselves to sleep.

And all the while, she stewed. She was far from home and unsafe. The scrap man might sell her in an eyeblink. He might let bent nose and lazy eye reach their filthy hands in. Who did she know in the world but Wife, Big Girl, the baby and the scrap man? She had a little money, but what if a shopkeeper suspected its source and called a constable? She had Irish, but what if the scrap man put word out that she was a thief? She had the length and breadth of the world to hide in, but where, exactly? A house? Where would she find a house? Would she live with others? Who would take her in? Would she be sent to school, a kid who couldn't read, add or write?

One concern outweighed all the others: the baby, the sister. Lily could not throw her to the wolves.

•

ANOTHER SUNDAY CAME and Lily awoke with a plan to ensure her safety.

The town was asleep, shut up and shut in. Grabbing a pair of wheat sacks, she rode to the nearest pub. It sprawled on a corner, its broad veranda hung with a dense grapevine that spooked her, the way it put out long, twisting strands to grab and throttle. The stink of Saturday drinking hung around the building. Tying Irish to a rail at the rear, where he could not be seen from the road, she went exploring, testing doors and windows, and there was a small window ajar, higher on the wall than any man. No ladder, no footholds, only Irish's broad back. 'Stay here, Irish,' she said, leading him beneath the window and using him as a platform while she pushed up on the worn, paint-peeling bottom frame, hoping it wouldn't stick.

The glass shot up with a bang. Lily waited, her heart pounding, for alarmed voices.

Nothing, but Irish was restless beneath her feet. She crouched, patted his neck, whispered, 'Stay, Irish,' and finally hoisted herself through the window. Darkness swallowing her up, she tumbled onto a lavatory floor. Oh, the unholy stink of that room.

Ten minutes later, she emerged, the wheat sacks clinking with unopened beer and sherry bottles. Then back to the mill, where she secreted the bottles here and there – in riverbank hollows, under scrap wood and dead leaves, among the dead bottles scattered all around.

The men were still asleep. She rode Irish out along the river road again to the house of the tea and rock buns. The round stone was where the scrap man had tossed it. She placed it on the gatepost and returned to the mill to wait for whatever nasty or cockeyed scheme the men cooked up.

•

SHE DIDN'T HAVE to wait long.

Midnight. Lily was asleep when she felt the wagon creak into motion. She crawled out from her bedding and there was Irish between the shafts, taking up the slack, and an unfamiliar shape on the seat, jerking the reins. 'Giddy-up.'

It was the man whose forehead she'd conked. 'What are you doing?'

He gave her a toothless grin. 'Won you at cards, missy. You, the horse, the wagon, fair and square. Giddy-up.'

They gained pace, edging along the wall until soon they'd be free of its pull. Passing an eyeless window, Lily glanced in and saw, in the ghastly light of the coals, two shapes flat out and snoring on the floor. Then the window slid by and she was mocked by the last bit of cold mossy stone.

She said, 'Isn't it too dark? Too cold? Why don't we leave in the morning?'

The swagman said, 'Ha!' at that. He flicked the reins, urging speed. 'Quit while you're ahead, that's my motto.' He half stood and jerked and whipped the reins, hurting Irish. 'Fucking nag, get a move on.'

The moment of fury forgotten, he gave her his grin again and said, 'And the grog's run out.'

Lily waited a few beats and put her hand on his foul sleeve. 'No, it's not. I know where my dad hides his bottles.'

The news travelled slowly through the man's brain. Easing Irish to a standstill, he cocked his head as if weighing the imperatives of his life: flee while he was the owner of a horse, a wagon and a girl, or stay and have another drink.

•

WHEN HE'D DRUNK himself to sleep, Lily rounded up the remaining half-dozen bottles and hid them in the wagon. Who knew when she might need them again? Then she poked and prodded the scrap man until he was dully awake.

'I lost you at poker,' he said presently, bewilderment written all over him.

'I don't care,' said Lily, dragging him to his feet and towards the door and the black night. 'Get a move on before they wake up.'

He jerked out of her grasp stubbornly. He staggered back to the dead fire.

'*No*,' wailed Lily.

But he was only going through their pockets and swags. He rejoined her, saying, 'Time to go.'

Isn't that what I've been saying? Lily thought.

Out into the cold air, which sobered him further, enough to climb aboard the wagon. 'You drive,' he said, and he fell into the tray and into sleep. Lily clicked her tongue at Irish – that's all you ever needed to do, you didn't need to force him – and soon he was taking them away from all of that.

•

A LONG TREK they had, back through the frosty weeks and along the ice-dotted roads of July and August. Gum trees, thrashed by the winds, sometimes lay across their path or tossed above their heads. Now and then Lily saw roadside and paddock daffodils nodding, yellow as if promising joy, but that was a lie. The clouds above them were torn scraps streaming across the sky and Irish struggled wherever the red soil plains had been rendered into mud. They came to creeks they could not ford, the water thundering, dead sheep carried in the froth and foam, fencing wire, trees and once a buggy. Lily was reminded of the flash flood at home, the peaceful little pools when it was over and the treasures they contained.

Throughout it all, the scrap man slept and she drove. If he woke to take the reins, or set up camp, or sell something from their dwindling supply of goods, he'd be puzzled, astounded. 'Where are we? What day is it?'

Lily couldn't give him the answers. She didn't know enough to say, 'We're near Bendigo,' or, 'It's Tuesday.' All she knew was they were on the road that passed the scar tree, and the day was one of the many still to be endured before they reached their stony acres.

And he'd taken to asking, 'Do you think her and the girl and the baby are all right? Enough food and that? Firewood?'

You've never cared before, Lily thought.

'We should of brought them with us,' the scrap man said, shaking his head.

One day, when his fretting threatened to spill over into fury, she gave him a bottle, and another. Placated, he went back to sleep, but she knew the peace would not hold. They needed to hurry.

•

A DAY CAME when they sold the last toasting fork and old-singlet cushion cover. The scrap man stared morosely into the tea caddy. 'We can't go home with hardly nuffink,' he said.

Lily didn't tell him about the paper money. She'd give it to Wife, who would know how to make it last. She got Irish rolling along and late that day they came to a bend in the road and a pub at the edge of a small flat town. Lily clicked her tongue, hoping Irish would hurry past, but the scrap man's senses always told him when a pub was close by, and he came crawling out from the mattress in the back. Grabbed the reins from her, his voice noxious in her ear: 'Not so fast.'

Lily slumped in defeat.

'What do you see?' he said.

She followed his grimy finger. Tied up at the pub were several horses and parked at the side a motley collection of sulkies, buggies, motor cars and a truck with a torn roof and stone-gouged knobbly tyres. Singing could be heard.

'We're gonna put your little fingers to work,' the scrap man said.

First they cleaned themselves. Parking the wagon in the rear yard, they found a tank with a tap on it and washed away the road dirt. The scrap man pulled on his best shirt, trousers and jacket, Lily beside him pinching her nostrils while she changed into the corduroy dress. He glanced at her critically and finger-combed her hair. He finger-combed his own.

The pub was cheery inside, men and women around tables or at the bar and children racing about. Through an archway a log fire glowed. How Lily wanted to stay a while, away from icy winds.

Before she knew it the scrap man had transformed himself into a fellow you wanted to spend time with. He slapped men on the back and bought a round of drinks. He told jokes and yarns. He caught the eye of the women and told them the one about the lady and her missing dog, '"Oh, have you seen my Titswaddle?" she cried.' He sat in for a round or two of cards, and won a little, lost a little, a threat to no one. He even led the room in a singalong around the fire. And all the while the air grew fumy with cigarette smoke and music and raucous voices, so that no one noticed the little girl in the burgundy dress and her quicksilver hands.

Lily stood at the shoulder of a man with a wallet in his gaping coat pocket as if to watch him play a few rounds of cards. He even winked at her and said, 'Gonna bring me luck, girlie?' as her thumb and forefinger eased out a ten-shilling note. She moved on to a table of knitting women who had stowed their handbags under their seats. Lingering a while as if drawn to the blur of their needles, she was very helpful whenever a ball of wool fell from a lap to the floor, ducking down to fetch it, one hand slipping into a handbag. She went everywhere, running around with the other children, tailing a woman to the lavatory, helping a man do magic tricks with the coins from his back pocket, always invisible, her hands quick and deft.

'Hurry,' breathed the scrap man when the publican called last drinks. He was pleased, terrified, gleeful. They were rolling in money. But it was time to run, people would be peering into their purses soon, patting their pockets.

•

AT LAST THEY reached the final track to the hut.

It was early spring, the grass all about thick and vivid, full of vigour and nodding with wildflowers. Birds carried nest-building mud and twigs in their beaks, ducks pecked and squabbled, kookaburras called and the days were longer and milder.

Lily and the scrap man trundled over the last rise and there was their hut in its hollow. Lily couldn't contain her joy. She had sorely missed the hut, the creek, the women, the baby. She hadn't had anyone to love until the baby had appeared. Even the scrap man wore a grin on his bushy face.

'Ahoy!' he shouted as they drew up.

The old horse sensed them first, stirring in the pen across the yard, whinnying to Irish, his ears alert. Then Wife emerged from the hut, shading her eyes. She managed a smile. Behind her came Big Girl and the baby, and the baby was so big now! A bright, alert being in Big Girl's skinny arms, looking at the newcomers in astonishment. Lily's heart lifted to see them, even as she could see from the women's reactions that their arrival was an incursion on happiness. A happy little knot of females for the past four months, and now look what the cat had dragged in.

1916

the sister

YEAR FOLLOWED UNCHANGING YEAR, EXCEPT THAT THE SCRAP man might vary the selling season as the fancy took him, the world was now at war – not that he noticed overall – and Lily grew more rooted to her family. To her *sister*; the others she endured. She hated being away from the little one. Out on the road with the scrap man, she pined, feeling for the child a careful and eternal appreciation. And the changes from one trip to the next! One moment a creature to cradle, the next a toddler taking her first steps with fierce, questing determination, and now three years old, a real character, quick, fluid and appealing. My sister, Lily marvelled.

Not that the scrap man noticed the child. Paying the little girl scant attention until she was old enough to walk and talk, he simply drummed into her the usual rules: No running away or he'd kill her, and watch out for the Social and the Education and their meddling ways. 'No talkin' to anyone what comes here, understand? Hide.'

So Lily was mother, father and older sister. Clearly the little one was loved in her absence, but it was distracted love. Life with the scrap man had shut down Wife and Big Girl. When he was away they were intent on survival. When he was home they were anxious.

•

THIS MORNING LILY crossed the yard in the dim light and entered the middle room of the hut, where Sister slept with Big Girl and Rosalind the doll. 'Wakey, wakey,' she whispered, gently shaking a bony shoulder.

Skinny, small, Sister nevertheless took up every inch of her grass mattress, her feet, hands and curls reaching into each corner. She seemed dead asleep but woke at once and flung her warm arms around Lily's neck.

Lily was overwhelmed. She held on tight before disengaging herself. 'Time to do the traps,' she whispered.

Sister slid from under the covers, padded across the floor to the crate where her clothes were stacked. She selected Lily's old corduroy dress, now thin, patched, faded and stained, pulled it over her head and stuck her feet in Lily's flappy old boots. She looked back at her bed uncertainly.

'Bring Rosalind,' Lily murmured.

Both horses snickered to see them, Irish stamping a hoof. Lily talked softly to him, stroked his neck, lifted Sister onto his back, finally led him out of the pen and across the yard to the creek.

Up the bank to the first trap. Sister wasn't a great help, too dreamy to take much in. And clearly Wife and Big Girl had done little to teach her how to set the traps, stun a live rabbit or peel and mount a skin. She would rather watch the ants, the eagles, the bees digging their heads into the wildflowers.

Seven rabbits this morning, five last night. With the carcasses hung from the saddle, the girls were in no hurry to return to the hut. They played games, naming objects and colours. Lily pointed at Irish's hide. 'I believe that's white?'

Sister shook her head solemnly. 'Brown.'

'White' was the patch on his forehead. 'Red' was the beading of blood on Lily's calf.

Other colours were tricky. How do you specify the blue-greyness of the hills on the horizon? The ginger tones on the farm cat that had appeared one day last year, streaking across the paddocks from the farmhouse to visit, purring, winding around their ankles. 'Cat,' Lily had said, for Sister had never seen a cat.

And here was the cat again. The girls, intent on drawing shapes in the dirt, heard the purring, felt the solid head butting against them. 'Cat!' said Sister.

But the cat was not alone. A voice said, 'Hello,' and a woman loomed over them, blocking the morning sun.

A number of complicated reactions ran through Lily's mind. *The lady does not want us to play with the cat. The lady does not want us to set traps along this creek. The lady knows we sneak in and steal her plums and strawberries. I am feeble-minded. Sister is feeble-minded. But who explains that if we're both feeble-minded? Where is the doll's house girl?*

They climbed to their feet. Sister's hand slid into Lily's.

'At your traps, I see.'

What could Lily say to that? It was self-evident. About the lady's head were wisps of hair. A canny smile on her face that was not quite kind. She wore an apron. Dust on her sturdy shoes.

She smiled at Sister. 'You're a pretty one.'

'She's feeble-minded,' Lily muttered.

The face sobered. 'Ah.'

The conversation petered out, the woman grabbing the cat and saying goodbye. 'I've got jam bubbling away on the stove.'

'We didn't make the cat come,' Lily said.

Another smile. 'Of course you didn't. He roams the countryside getting into mischief.' She gave Sister another searching look. 'Such lovely hazel eyes.'

Then she was gone and the little one had a name now, written across Lily's heart.

Lily crouched. 'Can you keep a secret?'

A solemn nod.

'Your name is Hazel. My name is Lily.'

'Lily.'

'Our secret,' Lily said.

•

ONE DAY WHEN the scrap man was away for a few days in his best suit and sly womanising smile, Wife returned from town with a rooster and a pair of hens in bamboo cages. Why not? She had money to spare now, demand for rabbit skins and carcasses being high, what with the war.

'Need a chook shed,' she told Lily and the others in her cut-short way.

They spent the rest of the day scrounging: fallen tree limbs as straight as they could find, old planks, chicken wire and tarpaulin rescued from the flash floods. The next morning they propped and tied and wired it all together and released the rooster and the hens into their new enclosure.

'Kitchen scraps,' Wife said.

They threw bits of bread and carrot peel to the chooks, Hazel squatting, absorbed, at the chicken wire, and the next morning they found two eggs in the straw nests under the wooden shelter. Scrambled eggs for breakfast one morning, boiled the next.

Then the scrap man came riding home, addled by drink and women, and he took one look at the new structure. 'Not made of money,' he raged.

Wife put her arm over her face. 'Sorry.'

'*I said, not made of money.*'

She took a step back from his risky fists. Lily stepped in. 'It's all scrounged,' she said.

'The chooks?'

'Hardly cost nothin',' Wife said.

'Saves us buyin' eggs,' Big Girl said.

They were ganging up and he wound himself tight – but he was also deeply fatigued. And he saw reason, as he sometimes did. That didn't stop him from circling the fowl house, however, running his expert scrutiny over it, dismissing it. 'One sneeze and the lot will come down,' he said, proceeding to point out the weak joints, the clumsy ties. 'Start again, stronger this time.'

They did, Hazel helping, the scrap man supervising, and now it was *his* fowl house. *He'd* built it. Just as he'd built the hut. The womenfolk shrugged. They were invisible. They sewed and stitched, made jam, twisted fencing wire, carted stones, made mortar from crowbarred dirt and bucketed bore water, nailed boards into place, but who noticed all that? Not the scrap man. They had hands tough as leather.

Admiring the structure now, the scrap man said, 'I'm tuckered out,' and he staggered off to his mattress.

•

BEFORE LONG A snore drifted across the yard from the hut, a nasty rip in the noontime air.

Wife cupped a hand to her ear dramatically. 'Listen!'

'What?' said the others, agog.

A gleam in Wife's eye. 'Is that a magpie I can hear?'

Only Hazel was puzzled. Lily and Big Girl were moment-arily shocked. Then the giggles took over.

Big Girl gasped, 'The piano?'

On still nights they could hear the farmhouse piano across the dry stubble, *do re mi fa so la ti do*.

They could scarcely hold it in. This was wickedness and they rarely got the chance to express it.

'Pigs at a trough?' offered Lily.

Wife gave it some thought. 'Pigs got more manners.'

Hazel eyed them as if she thought their ears needed rinsing. Then her face cleared. 'Irish,' she said, 'doing a fart,' and she ran giggling around the yard.

•

THE WEEKS PASSED, the daylight hours shrank, their stockpile of tinker's goods grew. There can't be a house in the land, thought Lily, that doesn't own one of our toasting forks. Or a second and a third because they soon break.

Otherwise the womenfolk continued to clear the stony acres, a task that offered no rewards. Dig out a stone, see another take its place. Cart the stones to the pile beside the house, go back for another load. 'We need a bigger place,' the scrap man had been saying. He was full of strenuous ambitions. He was a *landowner*, and landowners demanded fine dwellings for themselves. His ten acres of stones, dead tussocks, dirt and quartz reefs was a property, a farm, a holding. With a sly and natural satisfaction, he told his womenfolk to expect sheep grazing there one day. Ears of wheat rippling in a summer breeze. Admiring neighbours.

By a bigger place he meant a storeroom built onto the end of the hut. Starting as a patch of dirt, it grew higgledy-piggledy walls with gaps for a window and a door, and when the walls were at ceiling height he went away and came back with roofing iron and another window, God knows where from. He supervised; the womenfolk pushed, pulled, straightened, hammered nails, cut themselves on the rust-fringed iron, installed the window, hung a door of warped planks, the weeks passing so that it was spring before the scrap man stocked the storeroom with their tinker's wares and leftover wood, iron, wire and cloth.

the world war

LILY AND THE SCRAP MAN TRAVELLED THROUGH THE MILD spring days, stopping at farms and small clusters of houses that were towns only because there was a general store to anchor the people residing there. They did well, people responding to the man with his gallant charm, the shy pretty girl with a pictorial Bible in her lap – especially when it was known the pair were raising money and collecting donations for the war effort. Coins came tinkling in for Big Girl's napkins, Wife's chutneys, Lily's toasting forks. Woollen socks were donated, scrap iron, candlesticks, books, belts, cutlery. Well trained, Lily would turn a page of her Bible and the scrap man would murmur, 'She likes the pictures. Can't read or write. Can't talk, poor little mite.'

'Poor little mite,' the mugs would agree, and a few more coins would come his way.

One day they came to a cottage hard against a lonely track, a woman on her veranda swiping at the dust with a straw broom. 'That broom has had it,' observed the scrap man, checking over his shoulder that he had brooms for sale.

He stepped down from the wagon seat with his easy grace and doffed his hat, offering the smile he believed the women adored. 'Good morning, missus,' he said.

The woman eyed him expressionlessly, her iron-grey hair scraped back tightly and her dress almost to the ground like an olden-days figure. Lily, watching closely, saw that she carried a heartache of some kind. The scrap man could be depended upon not to spot it.

Instead, he began a prattle to soften her up. 'Bless you, missus,' he said, indicating the enamel brooch pinned to her breast, two bands of colour, purple over red, 'I see you're wearing the colours of the sixth battalion.' He knew all the colours by now. 'My brother is serving over there,' he added.

'My son,' the woman said.

'And I wish him godspeed until this awful mess is finished with,' the scrap man said. 'Now, forgive me for noticing, but that there broom of yours is on its last legs and –'

'He was killed,' the woman said.

The scrap man clutched his hat to his chest. 'Then may I say how dreadfully sorry I am to hear that. Right now I'm collecting for the –'

'I didn't come down in the last shower. You passed through here donkey's years ago and were out for yourself then, just like you are now,' the woman said – adding, with a last flick of her broom, 'Be off before I set the troopers on you.'

'Why didn't you tell me we were here before?' demanded the scrap man, returning rattled to his wagon seat.

Lily shrugged. By now, every town, every house, seemed indistinguishable from the one before it.

•

BUT LATER THAT week they reached a house that clearly they hadn't visited before. At the end of a long driveway edged with poplars was a huge pile dating from colonial times, two-storeyed, blank-faced but for the veranda wrapped around it like a skirt. 'There's money here,' crowed the scrap man.

Lily could see that. Stone stables, a groom in the sunlit entrance shoeing a horse. A garage with a gleaming black saloon. Sheds, hedges, pure white picket fences, a swept gravel forecourt delineated by stones painted white.

Hearing the wagon wheels crushing their costly gravel, two men emerged from the stable block. They must have been standing in the shadows watching the groom, Lily thought. Father and son, she guessed. Tall, loping men in jodhpurs and gleaming knee-high boots.

'Born to rule,' muttered the scrap man.

He stepped down, raised his hat. 'Good day to you, gentlemen.'

'May we help you?'

'I am here on behalf of the war effort,' the scrap man said. 'Any item that might be repaired or reworked or melted down to help our boys at the front.'

'The front,' spat the younger man.

Now that he was standing beside the wagon, Lily saw that he had one good eye and a milky dead one, the socket scarred and pulpy.

'Son,' the father said, touching the young man's forearm. Which was also scarred.

Now the father cocked his head to examine the wagon. 'Don't think I've seen your rig this way before.' He walked around to the rear, peered in. 'You've certainly amassed a great deal of scrap.'

'All for the war effort,' the scrap man said. 'I'm loading it on the Melbourne train tomorrow.'

'That's a fair old hike from here,' the father said.

'The day after,' the scrap man said.

'You fellows usually have your name painted on the side,' the man said, eyeing the faded canvas canopy, the gold and silver stars mere stains now. 'What's your name?'

Lily perked up. She didn't know the scrap man's name. She didn't know if he had one. A name had never been used or thought necessary. He was He, or Him.

He said, 'Paddy Holman.'

'Holman . . . Holman,' the older man said.

A change came over him. Rigid, shoulders back, he said, 'Holman. Is that a German name?'

The scrap man opened and closed his mouth.

The half-blind son said, 'And Paddy is Irish.'

Father and son stood side by side, stiff as statues. Pressure was building and they might explode. The scrap man danced on their gravel, *crunch, crunch*, lifting and setting down his boots, helpless against their hard hearts.

'I'm not German or Irish,' he said, placing his hand over his chest.

'I think you'd better leave, don't you?' the father said.

'Before we call the authorities,' the son said. 'Unless of course they are already on to you.'

When they were on the long return track the scrap man said fretfully, 'Keep your eyes open.'

And a short distance later, 'What name? What name?'

They reached the main road and it unfurled before them. Lily drove, the scrap man tried on names. He settled on 'Bert' and 'Jones' before the evening hours drew in. Bert Jones was no enemy alien.

That night for the first time he turned to Lily in the dark and told her a man had needs.

•

SHE AWOKE IN sticky, cramping pain and swamped by memories: his rank bulk toiling at her and sweet nothings in her ear. If that was love it had torn her open and was short-lived. He'd shuddered, peeling his flesh from hers long enough to say, 'Like a wet blanket,' before she was pinned there by the slumbering mass of him, couldn't breathe, his ripping snores.

She'd rolled out from under him and slept curled up in the grass and now, in the morning light, crept about too sore to straighten. She was ill-used, bewildered, broken at the wheel, but understood Wife's muttered wisdom, 'Keep your knees together.'

She sluiced off his traces and brooded through the long hours while the scrap man slept. She could run now, hoping he'd fail to hunt her down and kill her, or that a man from the Education or the Social wouldn't bring her back so he could kill her. But if she got away, could she hide, scavenge, steal, find a home? Her imagination let her down. She couldn't envisage any kind of future on her own. All she could see in her mind's eye was Hazel; Hazel part of the year in the hands of Wife and Big Girl, in whom tenderness was distracted and fearful, and part of the year on the road with the scrap man and his needs.

•

THEY SET OUT and the scrap man acknowledged nothing of the night, merely asked over and over again, what if a trooper stopped them? The wagon groaned from the weight of scrap metal and every corner overflowed: Big Girl's doilies, napkins and dresses; donated socks, mittens, mufflers, vests, pyjamas and shirts; cotton and linen offcuts and rags. At last a town appeared where the scrap man knew a dealer who would do them right.

They pulled into a yard beside the railway line at four in the afternoon and the dealer, a sly, gap-toothed, mouth-breathing trickle of water, cackled to see the scrap man again. Clapped him on the back and shook his hand and invited him in for a sherry.

'Stay with the wagon,' the scrap man said.

Lily did for five minutes but saw people gathering on the station platform, staring down the track, and then she heard a train rolling into town, the rails growling, air huffing and the whistle bleating. Hitching Irish to a post, she hobbled stiff and sore across the track and onto the platform as the train pulled in, steam and smoke swirling. She slid into the mass of men, women and children and for the first time no one was looking at her sideways and she didn't need to be some feeble-minded mute absorbed by Bible pictures. And she was strangely uplifted by the mood of the crowd. Only a train – but what a train.

The steam and the smoke cleared, revealing the engine and first carriage festooned with bright bold flags and banners. Lily couldn't read the words but the knobbly jointed boy next to her could. 'King and Country,' he murmured. 'Men Wanted. Enlist Now.'

Suddenly he turned to look at her. His eyes were bright and empty. He turned back to the train. There were soldiers aboard and –

'Told you to stay with the wagon,' snarled the scrap man, grabbing Lily's sleeve.

He grumbled all the way back across the tracks and the yard to Irish patiently waiting, how the dealer – 'lousy cow' – hadn't paid as much as expected.

'Sorry,' muttered Lily, for that was how you replied to his setbacks.

But the scrap man turned philosophical. 'Still, it's money in the pocket,' he said. 'And there'll be plenty of mugs walking around tomorrow.'

'That there is a recruitment train,' he explained, climbing aboard the wagon. 'Street fair tomorrow. Stalls. Parade. People flooding in from far and wide.'

Lily untied Irish and settled beside the scrap man, the seat worn smooth by their bums over the years. He clicked his tongue, flicked the reins, Irish began to move. Lily didn't know where they were going, where they were staying, but got a partial answer when they pulled up at a public lavatory behind the town hall. Unlacing his boots, the scrap man ordered her to scrape off the mud, rub in some wax, polish the toecaps with a rag. 'I'll be back in a tick.'

A woman or the pub or a poker game, she thought. And then he was emerging from the lavatory freshly shaved and with a spring in his step, wearing his best suitcoat, trousers with the purple braces and a whitish shirt. Handing him his boots, she wondered how long this time. All night? A day and a night? Several days? Several, if luck ran her way, but no good asking him his plans or intentions.

•

NOT THE PUB or a card game but a house where he was known by the woman at the door. He bowed, kissed the back of her hand and she wriggled her shoulders delightedly and slapped at him with a shrill laugh. He came back to Lily, said, 'You know what to do,' and turned back to the house, where he was swallowed up.

You know what to do. Those words had always been the signal for *Have a poke around.* Lily gazed at the now-closed front door. This was a town of houses on large blocks set back from broad streets. Behind the woman's house was a garden shed and a small structure that was not a cottage and not a garage or a stables but a cross between them.

Still slow and cramped, she began her search. The garden shed yielded a rake and a shovel, which she stowed in the wagon, keeping to the gathering shadows for fear the woman would crack open a blind or a curtain. The other building contained a single bed, bedside cupboard, wardrobe and cat-scratched armchair in the main section. Perhaps an unwanted relative had lived a banished life here at one time, but the place was stale now, the dust thick, the cobwebs hung with cobwebs. She passed the bed and the chair and found, curtained behind a sheet hanging from the ceiling, a nook crammed with crates, boxes, steamer trunks and suitcases.

She stepped in, letting the curtain fall, the dust to eddy, and picked through it all. Old coats and shoes, tattered books and magazines, cracked vases, a warped tennis racquet, tarnished silver goblets . . .

A doll's house.

It was small, grimy, the paint spider-webbed with cracks, but it was full of tiny, almost intact chairs, beds, cots and wardrobes. It was Hazel's size; Hazel who owned Rosalind the doll but almost nothing else.

•

LILY STOWED THE doll's house under a wheat bag in the wagon's tool locker. The scrap man had not rummaged in there for years. Then she waited, and the scrap man did not emerge, and evening drew in, so she explored the town and found tents, buggies, tethered horses and various cars and buckboards on the cricket ground at the edge of town. She manoeuvred the wagon past the crowded areas to a quiet corner, where she parked, unhitched Irish, took him to a trough to drink.

A stone clipped her bare leg, another struck her between the shoulders. She turned to face the danger or run and three boys said, 'Are youse Catholic? You look Catholic.'

They were her age, grinning with their arms back to throw again. A mother appeared from a tent and said, 'You boys stop that this instant,' the flat of her hand walloping a couple of behinds. But she did not say that she was sorry, or that the boys were sorry. She ignored Lily. To Lily it had been another attack out of nowhere and she knew all about those.

•

IN THE MORNING she drove out before those boys awoke to pack-roam with their stones and made her way to the woman's house. She waited a while. Presently she gave her piercing two-fingered whistle. Finally, with trepidation, she knocked.

The woman answered. 'He's not ready.'

Her hair was this way and that and one of the scrap man's mean, pinched cigarettes was in the corner of her smeared mouth. She wore a silk gown of fiery dragons, crusted food and cigarette burns, her rolls of skin barely contained and her face amused at Lily's discomfort.

'You're a tall one, aren'tcha.'

Lily said nothing.

'Pull the wagon into the driveway,' the woman said, then jerked her chin in the direction of the town centre. 'Head on down that way, you'll find marching bands and whatnot. He'll find you one way or another.'

When? Lily wanted to say.

•

FIRST SHE FILLED her fists with a few coins. Then, hanging on to them for dear life, she began to trudge in the direction indicated by the woman. As she neared the town centre, more and more people drifted from front gates and side streets until she had men, women and children in front of and behind her, all heading for the street fair. Some of the smaller boys wore soldiers' and sailors' uniforms, the girls were nurses. They all pressed on, Lily part of a throng. Even so, she was a different creature and they knew it. A boy sidled up and said, 'Who are you?'

'Lily.'

'Where are you from?'

She kept her eyes on the ground and kind of pointed west.

'You look strange.'

Stiff and sore, and not a nurse or a soldier or a freshly bathed daughter in ribbons and plaits but a waif in a nasty old dress and split shoes. She checked his hands: no stones.

He walked with her. 'Look at this.'

A medal pinned to his sailor's uniform. Where were his parents? Lily was panicked. 'Victorian Children's Patriotic

Fund,' he announced, tapping a fingertip to the medal. 'I collected five shillings.'

'Kitch! *Kitchener!*' snapped a woman behind them.

He waved goodbye and trotted back to his mother. Lily could feel them there, eyes boring through her spine.

She reached the town centre and stood, irresolute: flags, banners, streamers, a little bandstand with men playing oompah oompah tunes, stalls selling cakes and badges, children knitting socks and mittens. Presently the tug of curiosity and warmth drew her into the heart of it.

She had money – pennies, ha'pennies, a threepence and a sixpence. Spending a ha'penny, she bought a toffee apple; who could credit such a divine thing, sweet, crunchy and filling her empty belly? A penny and she had a paper bag of rock buns that would last her the day, except that she ate two of the six within an hour. Another ha'penny for lemon cordial in a tin cup ladled from a huge bucket, Lily required to drink it down on the spot and return the cup.

'Looks like you needed that, dear,' the woman said.

She had two children with her, a little soldier and a little nurse, both knitting scarfs. The boy ignored Lily but the girl had avid eyes for her, this girl in a tattered, too-short dress, gulping down lemon cordial as if to end a drought. Catching Lily's gaze, she stuck her tongue out.

'You're a tall one,' the woman said, eyeing Lily's inadequate hemline. 'Are you with your parents, dear?'

Lily waved vaguely at the bandstand. 'Over there.'

'I hope you haven't spent all your pocket money.'

Lily had heard this kind of thing all her life. Decoded, it was a demand to know where the money had come from. 'Never stole nothin',' she said, stalking off.

Except she *did* steal things, but that wasn't the point.

•

A PENNY REMAINED, the threepence, the sixpence. She walked on, swivelling her head left and right. Under that tent she might enlist in the army, at that table buy a war bond, in that clearing listen to a preacher, and over there write a postcard to a soldier at the front. But what she wanted to do more than anything was hit the Kaiser.

A man in a bowler hat, vest and bow tie shouted, 'Do your bit for the boys at the front – knock the Kaiser off his perch.'

He was juggling small wooden balls, red, green, yellow and blue and bruised all over, and Lily was transfixed by their rise and fall. He would stop, snatch them one by one from the air, soft thuds as they clacked together, and begin his juggling and his patter again: 'Roll up, roll up, hit the Kaiser today. A penny to knock him down.'

There were two Kaisers. The first was a large poster of a blockheaded man with a furious, pop-eyed, moustachioed monkey face, dressed in a spiked helmet and a high-collared coat. The second was a model fashioned from a stuffed chaff bag, coconut head and cardboard hat. It had been struck numerous times; chaff was leaking, the hat mashed, the white-paint cheeks and forehead half flaked away.

'Have a go, lass,' the man said, spotting the light in Lily's eyes but also playing to the boys in the crowd, who sniggered, expecting failure.

One penny got her three goes. Lily, bred on the stony acres, a slider through narrow gaps, a setter of traps and a puller of reins, had a strong arm and an unerring eye. She knocked the Kaiser off his perch three times and wiped the smirks from those faces.

She wandered on to the town hall, attracted by the movements of people in and out. There were banners on either side of the main doors, red crosses on white panels. She stepped in, seeing tables along one wall, piled with socks, mufflers, mittens, scraps of cloth and old clothing. Women worked side by side through the mess of it, sorting, saving, rejecting, having second thoughts. It was confusing to Lily. She, Wife and Big Girl made these things to hawk door to door in the assumption there was a dearth of them in the land, but here were enough to supply the whole world. She thought of the wagon and their unsold goods and supposed she should inform the scrap man.

Turning to leave, she noticed more women, some knitting, others feeding fabrics through sewing machines with a clatter and a whirr of the pedals, fast, slow, fast again. Even more proof of redundancy.

Hearing in the distance a bugle, she wandered back to the street. The oompah oompah band was gone, replaced by a row of stern, seated men with rosettes or medallions pinned to their suit lapels. Another man stood at the front of the stage and thundered at the people gathered to watch.

'Young man, are you wondering, *Why should I be asked to enlist? Is my country in peril?*' He paused, his eyes raking the crowd. He held up a stern finger. 'The answer, make no mistake, is a resounding *yes*.' He paused again, head cocked. 'Then why are you hanging back? Are you a coward? Are you a shirker?'

There were some in the crowd who didn't like his tack, but mostly there was a chest-swelling, his listeners lifting onto their toes with some urgency as he went on.

'*This is the time to do your bit,*' he cried. '*Make your way now to the recruiting tent.*'

He pointed, his whole arm quivering, and of course they all looked.

Lily went rigid. Two soldiers in khaki and gleaming leather boots, belts and straps sat at a table loaded with brochures and forms; one of them was the Social who'd come to the blue-stone mill, wearing an officer's cap. She backed away, seeking gaps in the crowd, but now the speaker was bellowing, 'Clear a path, please, clear a path, a hearty cheer for our recently enlisted local boys,' as a marching band emerged from a side street, leading a small troop of newly minted soldiers, barely out of boyhood.

Lily, trapped on the edge of the footpath, watched the little parade pass by. *Left, left, left, right, left* sounded the drums and the army boots stamping along. People began to clap, one or two whistled, but the soldiers did not waver. They drew near . . .

And suddenly Lily's heart began to flutter. Strange echoes. Ghost memories. That tall soldier. The particular configuration of his dimpled chin, long eyelashes and slightly hooked nose. Memories came swimming to the surface: the hut in the patch of dirt near the scrub line, the man and the woman and the many girls in plaits and the boys in bare feet, *this* boy a tall one now and boots and a uniform on.

As if he'd been shot with some kind of invisible ray, he turned his head and looked straight at her blazingly. His face cleared. New expressions chased across it: curiosity, bewilderment, loss, regret. Shaken, Lily thought: *He knows me.* Then he was gone, the little parade was gone and she was swept away on the tide.

•

STILL SHAKEN, SHE roamed the fair, not really seeing, hearing, registering. Of course she had no brother, only a brother dreamed up, beside a hut dreamed up. She had no past but a past invoked. And already that boy had been whisked out of her reach, she could not turn back the clock.

What woke her was the wagon, parked in a side street beside the town hall, Irish stamping impatiently in his harness. She stroked his damp, trembling neck, and then heard floating from a hall window the scrap man turning on the charm.

She went in. The Red Cross women were still knitting and sewing, sorting and stacking, but they were also keeping half an eye on a drama in the middle of the room where the scrap man was explaining to a large woman and a tiny one that any payment would be gratefully received, as it all went to the war effort.

Still wearing his best suit and jaunty hat, he was carrying a crate of goods. 'Table napkins,' he said, 'spatulas, socks, mittens, dresses.' Gesturing with it, he added, 'Whatever you can afford.'

'You don't understand,' said the tiny woman, a bundle of twigs, her hands on her hips. 'We don't *buy* items for the war effort, we are *given* them.'

'Ah, but doesn't a man deserve fair pay for the work he puts in?' argued the scrap man reasonably.

The big woman was not fooled by this debonair smiler. Bristling, she said, 'You look able-bodied. Why aren't you at the front? Are you a slacker?'

The scrap man looked wounded. 'Now listen here –'

'If you would like to leave your donation with us,' the small woman said hastily, 'it will be gratefully received.'

'A bunch of thieving –'

'Call the police, Violet,' the other woman said, and Lily slipped through to the scrap man rendered insensible by that word. 'Daddy, time to go,' she said, hooking his elbow with her hand.

He looked at her, astounded. A nasty little temper flared in his eyes, red eyes from drinking and womanising, his whiskers carelessly razored. But he could grasp some situations quickly and he smiled at the women and said forgive me, a misunderstanding, the family's waiting outside, keep up the good work, ladies.

At the wagon he said, 'Keep your eyes peeled,' and raged a while at the world.

Lily ignored him. She took the reins and clicked her tongue at Irish. They rolled on out and at the next town she tipped the crate of socks, mittens and flour-bag costumes in a Red Cross collection bin while he slept. Another day, another town, another bend in the road where a trooper might lie in wait – no wonder he was a man who every night had needs.

1919

peace

THIS TIME LILY AND THE SCRAP MAN MADE A SUMMER RUN through the back country and returned in February with many goods unsold and only a scattering of coins and a ten-shilling note. He was in a foul mood and stalked into the hut while Lily threw her arms around Hazel, now nearly six years old and full of curls and cheek.

He came storming out again, a few pennies in the palm of his hand. 'Where's the rest?'

Wife looked at the ground. 'That's all I got.'

'You spent it!' screamed the scrap man, kicking dirt up.

It was true that Wife and Big Girl had enjoyed the extra skin money. Alone during the selling months each year, no overseer to punish or berate them, they had grown close, like sisters, best friends, and had timidly branched out. They'd painted the kitchen chairs, for example. They wore shop-bought dresses.

'Didn't.'

'Didn't,' echoed Big Girl, who was pregnant again.

'Wasn't talkin' to you.' He closed in on Wife with a punch that felled her to the ground and rattled her teeth. 'You're hidin' it from me.'

She looked up at him from the dirt and said through bloody spit, 'Mr Anderson said demand's fallen.'

'Demand's fallen? What're you talkin' about?' said the scrap man in bewildered wrath.

'Demand for skins and that,' Wife said. 'Now the war's over.'

This was double Dutch to the scrap man. He scarcely knew the war was over or that there had been a war.

Seeing his doubt, Wife rolled away from his boots and climbed to her feet. 'He's buyin' less. He can't pay as much.'

The scrap man turned to Lily and snarled, 'Termorrer *you* go to town with the skins.'

As if she would get at the truth. A trip to town by herself . . . People, shops, independence for a couple of hours. For a fleeting moment Lily thought she might run. Ride Irish into town, sell the skins and carcasses, ride on out the other side. Or catch a train.

But the scrap man would kill her if she ran again, or mould Hazel into something awful to contemplate.

•

WHEN THE TIME came, Lily asked if Hazel could accompany her.

'You think I'm stupid?' sneered the scrap man. 'She's the only thing keepin' you here.'

So he wasn't stupid. And it had been a long shot. Lily shrugged, hitched Irish to the buggy and trundled out along the track.

One hour to town. She was seeing it with fresh eyes, alone, in charge, but it wasn't much of a place, crouching under cheerless gum trees and broad, sun-faded verandas, waiting for something to happen. The Melbourne train came through once a day, most days, otherwise there was no reason for a town to exist, let alone a skin buyer with a warehouse beside the tracks.

She found Mr Anderson standing with his assistant in the front yard of his business. They seemed to have time on their hands, and watched Lily's arrival with indifference, before Anderson sighed and crossed to the buggy.

'I'm not buyin' today.'

Lily explained that she'd driven many miles. Her father would be disappointed. 'They's good skins.'

Anderson, tall, whiskery, gauntly sad, stared at the skins she'd stacked in the little compartment behind her seat. 'Demand's down, the war's over. The army has no need of hats, coats, what have you.'

'Please, sir.'

His face twisted in anguish, he tipped a few coins into her palm. 'There. Satisfied?'

He stalked off to his office.

The other man helped Lily unload. He was a tough little knot of muscles with a mouth as tight as a purse. He hadn't shaved, or had shaved in the dark, and smelled and looked greasy. Lily breathed shallowly. That made her cough.

The assistant went very still. 'You got the flu?'

Lily frowned. 'No.'

'It's going around,' he said.

They worked in silence, Lily finally turning away to climb aboard the buggy. The assistant watched her, his hands on his hips. 'You got quite a nerve, you know.'

'Beg pardon?'

'The boss lost one son in the war and the other come back with mustard gas in his lungs and you turn up like butter wouldn't melt in your mouth.'

Lily said nothing, hiding her confusion. She got out of there, roamed the streets for a while. She saw a passing car, a man with a cartload of hay, a woman with a shopping basket, but that was it, the town slumbered. Wife wanted tea and flour. The shopkeeper served her wordlessly; she was the only customer. On the way out she passed the Mechanics' Institute, where a man in a khaki coat sat on a stone bench in the sun. He'd lost an arm, the empty sleeve was pinned across his chest, and as she went by she felt reproved, as though condemned for having all she needed in life.

She returned to the hut with her tea, flour and her fistful of coins and got in first, jutting her chin at the scrap man, saying, 'That's all he paid.'

She'd learned over time that if she were stern and unavailing it might put him on the back foot. 'I was lucky to get it,' she went on. 'He said no one wants rabbit skins now the war's over.'

He went red, mottled, struggled with his temper. Finally he nodded his head at the tea and the flour, telling her in his stunted way to unload.

•

BUT LILY'S REPORT put him in a thoughtful mood, and next day he muttered around the cigarette in the corner of his mouth, 'You, come with me.'

Lily left off sharpening a toasting fork prong and followed him into the kitchen, where Big Girl was ostensibly showing Hazel how to peel potatoes. One potato sat on the cutting board, a greenish-white globe damply finger-marked by muddy little hands, but Hazel's doll's house was also on the bench and peeling one potato was the extent of her interest. Pointing at Hazel, the scrap man growled, 'You.'

She jumped in fright. Glued herself to Big Girl's thigh.

Lily watched him uneasily. He'd drained all of his sherry bottles days ago and hadn't been back for more, and a sober scrap man was an unhappy one. Drunk or sober, he was mean and unpredictable.

But it seemed he hadn't punishment in mind. Sticking his face into Hazel's he said, 'Time to learn you a few things,' the cigarette bobbing in his mouth.

Lily and Hazel followed him outside and around to the new storeroom. 'Get in there.'

He shoved them towards the window, which was in two sections, a fixed upper pane and a sliding lower pane, latched where the two met. It was currently latched, the scrap man fearing thieves. 'Learn her everyfink I learnt *you*,' he told Lily.

She understood. She had been fearing this day, trying not to imagine it, but it was here now and a complicated feeling settled in her. For years she'd been the scrap man's best little thief and pickpocket, praise he gave grudgingly. For years she'd been a slip of a thing, easily overlooked, able to flick unnoticed through windows and slip her fingers into a pocket or purse without disturbing fabric or nerve cells. But she'd shot up in height, she was tall like her brother the soldier, and on the last trip she'd got stuck in a bathroom window and a woman knitting in a pub had told her, 'Move away, you're making me uncomfortable.' The scrap man had taken to giving Lily hard, assessing looks after that. Eventually he'd said what was on his mind: 'Reckon you're getting too big for this caper.'

'Everyfink I learnt you,' he repeated.

Except he *hadn't* taught Lily how to thieve and pickpocket. Big Girl had. And Wife had taught Big Girl.

Lily's thoughts were all messed up. After she'd trained Hazel, would she be left behind, shunted to the side? That hurt. She didn't want to be unneeded. She didn't want Hazel to be his best girl. She felt jealous and hateful and fearful all at once. The thought of Hazel, the one she loved, *alone on the road with him.*

'Whatcha waitin' for? Get a move on.'

Lily touched her sister's forearm, pointed at the latch, gave a little head jerk. Hazel knew how to read the family's head jerks, and, reaching up on the grimy soles of her feet, flicked open the latch. Then, glancing at Lily for confirmation, she tucked her fingers under the two handles and lifted the lower pane until a gap appeared between glass and sill and sweet air poured in.

Lily smiled, nodded and closed and latched the window again. She hoisted Hazel onto one hip, the better to see, and demonstrated the latch's simple action. Setting Hazel down again she said, 'Now I'll show you how to open it from the other side.'

They trooped out and around to the patch of dead grass beneath the window. The scrap man proffered his pocketknife. Lily opened a blade.

'Let me, let me,' Hazel said with a skip in the dust.

Lily gave her the knife handle-first. 'This is how you hand someone a knife.'

'Get on with it,' the scrap man said.

Hazel stepped up to the window. She inserted the blade, flipped open the latch. But then looked puzzled. How to lift the windowpane? There were no handles here on the outside, and the bottom edge was seated inside the frame. She glanced at Lily. Lily glanced meaningfully at the knife.

Hazel understood. She angled the blade until it gained purchase under the pane and levered upwards until a gap appeared, then used her fingers to widen it.

'They won't always slide so easy,' the scrap man said. 'Now climb in.'

Hazel hooked her fingers on the sill and pulled and scrabbled until her trunk was through the gap. Lily wanted to give a boost but had anyone ever boosted her? And the scrap man would only get cranky.

•

WITHIN A WEEK, Hazel could slip in and out of the window as though barely disturbing the air.

'Pockets,' grunted the scrap man.

So Lily taught the little one the art of sliding her hand into the secret folds where people carried their coins, purses and wallets: hip and bum trouser pockets; inner and outer coat pockets; handbags; knitting bags; suitcases; sleeves. She posed the scrap man, Wife and Big Girl in all the situations she herself had faced. She had them sit at tables while Hazel sidled in. She had them stand still, stand restlessly, stroll along. She had them lie supine as though basking in a grassy park.

Hazel's ability wasn't the problem, it was the scrap man's hypervigilance. He knew she'd be sliding her hand into his pocket, and so of course he always felt the motion of her fingers, felt his wallet catch on the stitching of his pockets. Backhanding her across the face, he'd straddle her where she lay in the dirt and growl, 'Stupid girl, do it again.'

One day, risking a black eye herself, Wife said, 'You'll give her butterfingers.'

The scrap man went tense, red, explosive, but at the last moment took a deep breath and helped Hazel to her feet. Brushed off the dust. Patted her head in a ghastly approximation of tenderness. 'Try again.'

Pretending to be a bloke propping up the main bar of some pub, he rested his forearms on the wagon tray and began a tuneless whistling. But there was expectation in his back. He could sense Hazel coming in on his left flank, quivering with nerves.

That's when Lily moved. She came in on his right and began a conversation.

'When're we goin' on the road again?'

The scrap man looked at her in suspicion and astonishment. After a while he said, 'Middle of the year.'

'All of us?'

He shook his head. 'You, me, the little one.'

'Wheel's broke,' Lily reminded him.

A broken spoke in the left-hand rear wagon wheel. 'I'll fix it,' the scrap man snarled. Why was she talking to him? He didn't like or trust or understand it.

'Got it!' shouted Hazel.

He turned. She had his wallet. She waved it at him, grinning, a few steps out of the range of his fists and boots. Lily watched him anxiously. She could see in his madness a desire to beat Hazel for fooling him, but sanity returned as it did from time to time and he grimaced. If you didn't know him you'd mistake it for a smile.

'You're a corker, my best little housebreaker and pickpocket.'

Because I distracted you, thought Lily grumpily.

•

SHE STEWED ABOUT it. She felt pushed and pulled. *She* had been the best, the scrap man had told her so. But praise from him was scanty. Would he ever tell her she was his best little rabbit-trapper and -skinner? His best little sewer and stitcher? Best little bender of wire and snipper of tin?

But mostly Lily fumed because she began to see that she was nothing but a stage in a process, and so was Hazel. One day Hazel would outgrow windows and pockets, so another girl would be trained in thievery. Or boy. What if Big Girl had a boy? Lily looked at that from all angles and decided it wouldn't matter to the scrap man. A boy would be his slave as much as any girl. Love in this family was inconvenient, insupportable and unwelcome. No one knew precisely what love was. All Lily knew was that she loved Hazel. Hazel, her sister, a receptacle of love.

Clouded with doubt, she cast glances at Hazel as they gutted and skinned that afternoon. Was there anything uniquely her own that she could pass on? All she could offer Hazel were bits and pieces of knowledge that went unnoticed and unremarked by the rest of the world. Like squatting to view the busyness of the ants.

Today the ants happened to be going crazy in the red dirt. 'Look,' she said.

Hazel crouched with her. 'Do they bite?'

'Yes.'

Lily glanced uneasily towards the house. Ant-gazing was bound to rile him. Turning back to Hazel she pointed at an ant carrying a crumb to a hole in the ground. 'Food.'

Hazel said presently, 'Like a storeroom.'

'When they race around like this it's going to rain.'

They craned their necks to the sky, which was clear. 'When?'

'Tonight. Tomorrow.'

They finished their chores and before the light fled from the sky Lily taught Hazel how to make a daisy chain from some flowering weeds. Next day she showed her how to identify the types of tree bark that concealed the grubs that worked best as yabby lures. The day after that, how to think like a chook and find where they lay their eggs when they were allowed to roam the yard. How not to look at a storm. How to cross your fingers to ward off misfortune. That the ghost of the old dog roamed on the track behind the stone house, and ghost people still lived along the creek but would do her no harm. All these things and more. As if they might secure her sister against the future.

•

SHE COULDN'T SECURE herself against her own future. She was transforming, the alterations irreversible. Wispy hairs appeared. Her nipples troubled her: sensitivity, discomfort. Feelings she couldn't name. And the scrap man came to her often, boarding the wagon, boarding her. He would stick his thing in, twitch, moan and fall asleep while she, in her mind, roamed over the hills and far away.

•

SHE WOULD AWAKE feeling bruised and sticky, slip out from under his arm and wash it all away before taking Hazel along the traps. They'd return, feed and water Irish, comb the burrs and clotted mud from his coat, tail and mane, skin and gut the rabbits, head at last to the hut. The yard was always silent at that hour. No smoke rose, no movement of any kind, only a hint of eucalyptus as the sun alighted on the gum trees. It had become Lily's job to get the coals burning in the firebox, water muttering in the kettle, dripping to spit in the frying pan.

This morning, trailed by Hazel, she stepped through the door on its leather hinges and felt the stovetop. Still warm from last night. Opening the firebox, she prodded the embers and added a mix of coal, bark, twigs, pine cones and the newspaper scrap the shop butter had come in. Lily still couldn't read – the type crawled like ants across the page – but she could read a photograph clearly enough. This one was small, grainy, showing a street, a shopfront and some solemn men and women staring at the camera. A few wore white masks over their faces and Lily felt spooked. She shuddered involuntarily.

When the water was boiling she brewed tea in a big dented pot. She showed Hazel how to break eggs into the frying pan, add lamb's fry and strips of bacon. Hazel watched, still and silent now, cowed by the house. The house was a place of eruptions you couldn't predict.

Big Girl emerged first. Her resources drained by her pregnancy, she shuffled everywhere, stripped of hope or power. Then Wife emerged, rubbing her eyes, and both women sat at the table, which was a warped wooden door sitting on almost-straight legs from a storm-toppled gum tree. Who knew where the door had come from? They'd thought he was out drinking and whoring one day and he'd come back with a door. It was ringed and sticky with sauce, candle wax, sugar and sherry, so you minded where you rested your forearms.

Seeing how stiffly Lily held herself – at the stove, delivering the plates and sliding onto the long bench seat – Wife murmured, 'It's no good fightin' him.'

Lily blinked. Everyone knew the scrap man visited her in the night as much as he did the others, but it had never been acknowledged. Pull a long face and carry on, they all knew the truth of that.

Besides, she didn't fight him, and would not. It was just that he took her as if she were fighting him. As if to underscore that, suddenly the scrap man was in the doorway, slack-jawed, half-buttoned, his hair greasy, knotted and combed by a cat again.

He shot them suspicious looks. Hazel darted onto the bench beside Lily. They waited, watching his fists, but the walk from Lily's wagon-tray bed had tired him and his womenfolk were a blur that early in the morning. He slumped at the table and said, 'Breakfast.'

The others ate quickly, sparingly, and fled from the table, leaving Wife to tend to his needs. It was a day like all of the others: fencing wire, wire cutters, tinsnips, cotton rags, scissors and spools of thread awaited them on the patch of dirt beneath the tarpaulin shade.

•

ANOTHER DAY DAWNED, Lily waking at rooster crow. She threw off the scrap man's arm, pulled on a dress and boots, collected Hazel, who this morning slept curled around the doll's house. The girls were stunned, as always, by the early hour, the half-light. Every action was wordless, their first thirty minutes of each day: crossing the yard, saddling Irish, heading out with him to run the line of traps along the creek bank.

Only four rabbits this morning, but a nose-searing stench aroused their curiosity. A dead rabbit beside the fence, days old, a chewed-up mess of fur and splintered bone. Lily got closer, peering down. Hazel crouched, pinching her nostrils. 'Pooh!'

'Fox got it,' Lily said.

Hazel's grunt said she didn't know what a fox was.

'Like a dog,' Lily said. 'They eat rabbits and lambs.'

Bad news for the scrap man. They walked Irish back to his pen, gutted and skinned the rabbits. No sign of the women-folk. No sign of the scrap man, only his snores. The sun, still low on the eastern horizon, promised a basking kind of warmth today. Lily was starving. 'Eggs.'

On a good day they'd find four or five eggs in the fowl house or in the secret places the hens found around the yard. Fried eggs on toast every day, Lily's favourite meal. Hazel close on her heels, she entered the chook yard and scattered a mess of kitchen scraps onto the dirt. Hens, rooster and two new chicks came racing, tangling and pecking.

Hazel gaped at the chicks. 'Babies!'

Very new, Lily thought. This morning or last night and already behaving like hens. She edged around them and into the shelter, finding three eggs, two in one nest of still-warm straw, one in another. Small, brownish-white, shit-smeared.

She returned to Hazel, who crouched with her hands cupping her jaw, watching the chicks. 'Where did they come from?'

'Eggs.'

Hazel glanced in horror at the eggs in Lily's hands. 'We eat babies?'

'Only some eggs become chickens,' Lily said, but that was the extent of her knowledge, passed on by Wife.

Trying to put down layers of harmony and trust, she added, 'We wouldn't hurt babies.'

Hazel was confounded. She walked silently with Lily across the yard to the kitchen and was mute while Lily stoked the coals and melted dripping in the frying pan. Then Big Girl waddled out, yawning and scratching, her belly pressing hard against her flour-bag nightgown.

Hazel stared at the belly. Her hand shot out, forefinger quivering. 'Baby?'

Big Girl grunted assent, a sleepy smile and pregnancy tiredness in her face.

Hazel said, 'Will I get a baby too?'

'One day.'

'Where did yours come from?'

Confusion crept over Big Girl in an unwelcome tide. She stammered that she didn't know. She turned afflicted eyes to Lily and said again, 'I don't know. It just came.'

Help me, her expression said.

Lily didn't know either. 'Babies just come,' she said, cracking the first egg on the edge of the pan while over in the wagon the scrap man slept on.

•

THREE TRAPPED RABBITS one day, two the next, two again, then five, and one day none at all. So it was even more pointless to make regular trips to the skin buyer as Wife had done in the early war years. Nowadays she made one trip a week, with twenty skins if they were lucky – not that Mr Anderson could pay much.

There came a time when Wife appeared at the breakfast table with her arm in a sling. No one asked her why. Last month a closed eye, half her face a purple bruise. Last year a broken collarbone. A bad knee, another black eye, cracked ribs, back through the years that Lily had known her. She'd say, 'Accident,' the scrap man would say, 'Accident.'

But it was getting worse.

Wife sat at the table, wouldn't look up as Lily slid a plate of scrambled eggs before her. Then the scrap man appeared, yawning, scratching, collapsing at the table. 'I need you to help her' – a head jerk to indicate Wife – 'take the skins in today. She fell over and buggered her arm.'

Why don't *you* help her take the skins to town? thought Lily crossly. But she knew why not: he feared if Lily were left unguarded on the stony acres she'd run. Take the others and run.

Lily and Wife set out, one hour to town, one hour back, along empty potholed roads and through shimmering mirages. Harvest long over, the stubbled paddocks stretched to the horizon with only an occasional rooftop and smudges of garden and windbreak trees to stand in relief against a dusty world. Fat clouds sat; otherwise the sky was a great blue dome. Heat-stunned birds squatted on the wires and skinny sheep followed each other head to tail along well-trodden paths through the dead grass. There was no wind and the tanks and troughs were dry. February. Hot. And today Lily was feeling a bloated, aching heaviness low in her stomach. She couldn't have made a run for it if she tried.

Hearing the horse, buggy, Lily and Wife arrive with a weary creaking, Mr Anderson's snarly assistant stepped out into the daylight and shaded his eyes. For some reason a scrap of grubby white cloth was tied around his neck.

'You,' he said, staring glumly. He lifted the cloth until it masked his nose and mouth. 'I want youse to keep your distance,' he said, his voice muffled. 'You got the flu?'

Lily and Wife exchanged puzzled glances. 'No.'

'Still,' he said, 'stay where you are.'

Keeping well clear, he eyed and counted the skins. Lily couldn't read his face but she did read his eyes. Canniness seeped in, as if he sensed their awful need. 'I can only give youse a couple of bob.'

As if visualising the scrap man an hour from now, Wife said with a nervy, constricted laugh, 'Mr Anderson pays more than that.'

'And I don't. It's *my* business now.'

The cotton mask muffled his scorn. His glance, lingering on Lily, took on a creepy darkness. As if she might sweeten some deal he had in mind, he said, 'I'll go as high as two and threepence . . . unless you're sellin' somethin' else?'

Lily tried to stare him down. 'Three bob.'

'Don't make me laugh,' he said with pitiless force. 'Two shillings and threepence, take it or leave it.'

To conceal her distress, Wife coughed and blew her nose and gave the appearance of a woman who could take it or leave it.

'You got the flu?' demanded the skin buyer again, taking a step back.

'No. Two and nine,' Wife said.

GARRY DISHER

The man looked at the ground, patiently shook his head. 'Two and six.'

'Two and nine,' said Lily.

'Two and six.'

Wife, in her helpless longing, said, 'All right.'

He dug in his greasy pants and counted out the money. He wouldn't come near Wife and Lily but plonked the coins down on top of the loading dock and, looking small, nasty and triumphant, scooped up the skins and disappeared.

•

THE FACE MASK, his odd behaviour, the measly price . . . it cast a pall over Lily and Wife. They trundled in the cart back through the town, the short main street with its bank, general store, post office, pub and not much else. Lily saw the one-armed soldier again, this time sitting on the edge of a shop veranda with his feet in the gutter, his face seeking the sun as if he needed to thaw from the grip of an icy no-man's-land. Past the Mechanics' Institute where a raw new statue had been erected, a carved white soldier standing with his slouch hat aimed piously at his feet, a downturned rifle between his legs. He was so new the birds hadn't pooped on him. A brass plate on the plinth and a list of names.

Even Irish was sunk in gloom. He plodded in sullenly to the edge of the town, where tattered hedges gave way to rusty fences and acres of sparse, dusty stubble. Bar the squeaking

144

of the cart wheels, the clopping hooves, a scrappy bird above their heads, the air was still and soundless.

Lily was lost in dreams. She visualised Hazel, a ribbon of colour in the dry sameness of the summery world. White teeth, tossing auburn hair and fleet white heels. Concentrating hard, giving the image houseroom, she pondered life *without* Hazel. There would be an almighty hole inside her. Hazel filled her up where Wife and Big Girl never had.

She was distracted by a sensation of wet stickiness between her legs. She pulled up the hem of her thin cast-off dress, peered at herself. An awful new vivid colour. Blood, thickly dark, in the crotch of her hand-me-down underpants.

She gasped, shoved the hem down over her knees again and cringed in wetness. She wanted to sink into a river. There was a faint rich smell about her and no sharp pain, not like when the scrap man tore her open that first time in the night, so what accounted for the blood?

Her heart pounding, she lifted the hem again and said, 'I'm bleeding.'

Wife, startled from some wagon-riding reverie of her own, peered at her. A slow, unavailing smile came over her wooden face, a kind of unpleasant we're-in-the-same-boat expression. 'It's your monthly,' she said, as if that made it all clear.

•

THEY REACHED THE stony acres and, in her wretchedness, Lily raced to the bore with a bucket, a sponge and a change of clothes while Wife was berated for coming home with two and sixpence.

Lily's blood kept on coming.

Presently Big Girl appeared with a scrap of old singlet. 'You need to wear a rag.'

Lily felt undermined. Such bleeding happened to Wife and Big Girl, not her. 'Always?'

'When it's full, swap it for a clean one.'

'Forever?'

'Few days,' grunted Big Girl. 'Same again next month.'

Mute, helpless, Lily folded the cotton piece into her change of pants and pulled them up. Now she felt stickily padded and was inclined to waddle when she walked. The shame was scorching. There was a smear of blood on her inner thigh, blood drying on her hands and in dark crescents in her fingernails. She cast about for fresh water but it was bloody water and she'd have to start again. She didn't know where to start.

The scrap man wandered up, a fresh torment in her life. 'It true?' he demanded.

Was what true? That she'd bled? Lily said nothing, which inflamed him.

'Only two and six?' he yelled.

Relieved, angry, Lily put her shame aside and said, with chilly disparagement, 'Yes.'

He glowered, slapped her and wandered back across the yard to the storeroom, which swallowed him up. Clinks and thuds as he searched without hope for one of his bottles.

Big Girl said, 'At least you're not pregnant,' whatever that had to do with anything.

•

AS IF SECRETLY afraid it was all slipping away from him, the scrap man stirred the womenfolk with a fierce new relish. 'There's always a mug ready to hand over his money,' he stormed, pacing up and down, pinching, twisting earlobes, urging them to get a move on, more spatulas, more toasting forks, more flour-bag dresses and petticoats. And they would get a move on, their heads down to forestall chaos and pain. It was never enough of course.

One day Lily happened to glance at a length of fencing wire with fresh eyes. She picked it up, bent one end, the other, until she had two jutting elbows and a hook. In her mind's eye, a coat hung from this clumsy gadget. She tested it on Wife's old coat, hanging it from a tree.

The scrap man wandered over eventually, in his heavy, unswerving way. He frowned at the apparition. Light dawning, he took his smoke from his mouth. 'Coathangers,' he said. 'Clever girl.'

Lily wriggled her shoulders. Praise from him was rare, imponderable. Fevered and provoked by it, she tried to visualise other ways to adapt the scrap everywhere around them, the cast-off tins, boxes, bottles, wire and clothing. She drilled holes in the lid of a tobacco tin, filled the tin with soap flakes and called it a soap shaker. Cut slits in a small piece of roofing iron and called it a cheese grater. Bound thick strips of corduroy to a headless broom handle and called it a mop.

And so the weeks passed, the women toiling through the shortening days, in a queer grey light under muttering skies. The autumn rains were expected and the scrap man was eager to start selling and trading again. 'Move,' he'd say.

They bent their backs. Their hands flew, snipping, twisting, hammering, stitching. They ached. Their fingers bled. All through the hours and days they were alert to his moods and absences. If he stumbled off in search of grog or a card game, he always returned. If he disappeared into the hut to drink or sleep, he always staggered out again.

But when he was away, for a few precious minutes or hours, the women whispered, giggled, wished him dead. These were their best times. Lily felt them powerfully, these snatched moments, Hazel close beside her, a sweetly unguarded presence, a quick, fluid, powerfully loved presence.

•

ONE DAY A voice said, 'Hello there.'

They stilled their busy hands to dart a look at the visitor and then for signs of the scrap man, expecting his wrath, but he was moving boxes over in the storeroom. 'Keeping busy?' the visitor said.

It was the woman who owned the cat, accompanied by a girl of Lily's age. A pair of subtle intruders, they must have come to the stony acres on soft footfall, over their paddocks and down along the creek and, finally, across the scrap man's yard. We're in trouble, thought Lily. They know we pinch their tomatoes, strawberries and plums. Wife and Big Girl, badly panicked, shot looks at Lily as though they saw in her the authority to deal with this.

'Hello,' Lily said.

'Such industry!' marvelled the woman.

She had a long, searching nose. It was built for smelling rats, tricks and badness. She eyed the completed and half-completed toasting forks and flour-bag smocks, the leftover scraps, the tools and sore fingers. Lily eyed her uneasily, this woman who had bestowed on Hazel a name but was now looming over them like a beady-eyed crow.

Unable to withstand those eyes, Lily glanced at the girl and recognised the crosspatch doll's house wrecker, older now, and clearly enjoying Lily's discomposure. She smiled at Lily, a discrediting smile, full of secret judgements and satisfactions. Lily looked away, wary and hurt.

'And the little one,' cried the woman, crouching with a puff of flowery perfume from the neck of her dress to rake Hazel with her eyes. 'My goodness, look at the state of those fingers!'

Hazel shrank away, her shoulder hard against Lily's, the doll Rosalind clutched to her chest.

'She's feeble-minded,' whispered Lily in agitation. Where was the scrap man when you needed him?

'Fiddlesticks,' the woman said.

'She is too,' Big Girl retorted, shifting her unwieldy shape on the ground cloth, rubbing her stomach. With the baby so big now, any configuration of her body was unendurable, any bending, reclining, standing or walking.

The farmer's wife snorted. She stood, her joints creaking. Staring fixedly at Hazel, she said, 'This child should be at school.'

Wife muttered, 'You can't learn her nuffink. She's not right in the head.'

They all wanted the woman to leave. They feared the scrap man.

'Rubbish,' the woman replied. 'She's perfectly sound. You can see it in her eyes. And fair warning, I have spoken to the authorities about the situation here.'

Behind her the girl continued to give Lily a sly, unyielding smile. Lily looked away.

The woman wasn't finished. She loomed over them implacably. 'Spell cat,' she demanded of Wife.

'Er,' Wife said, her eyes darting about.

'Two twos,' snapped the woman at Big Girl.

Big Girl slumped, bruised and indeterminate, as if she might cry.

Inflamed now, exultant, the woman turned to Lily. 'What year was the Battle of Hastings?'

Lily stared at her. She must have looked clever and durable to the farmer's wife, who went on unstoppably: 'I don't believe *any* of you has had *any* schooling. You camp here, coming and going like gypsies, free as you like. You steal from honest, hard-working people and never wash or go to school or church. It's a disgrace.'

The scrap man came strolling across the yard, finger-combing his hair, directing his charmer's smile at the newcomers. 'Good day to you, missus.'

Lily could see the panic and unease behind it. The woman might bring the authorities down on them. 'And good day to you, young lady,' he said.

The girl shrank back, let herself be shielded by her mother. Who drew herself up like a peacock and said, 'It's disgraceful, putting these little girls to work like this. They should be in school.'

'It's Sunday,' the scrap man said.

'You know what I mean. These children have had no education from what I can see.'

'You can't get nothing out of them. Not right in the head. Backward.'

'Don't be ridiculous.'

The scrap man bristled. 'Who are you calling ridiculous?'

The daughter came from behind her mother's skirt to say, 'Pooh, you stink.'

'The pair of you get off my land,' the scrap man said.

With an air of imparting a vital truth, the woman said, 'You haven't heard the end of this.' She pointed at Hazel. 'I'll see that child is made a ward of the state.'

She turned to go, tugging her daughter by the hand, the daughter casting Lily a last smirk.

•

THE SCRAP MAN shook his fist at their departing backs, but flew into a dither as soon as they were out of sight. 'Stop what you're doin' and load the wagon,' he yelled. 'Hitch the damn horse.'

He pointed at Wife and Big Girl. 'You two are stayin' here.'

Pointed at Lily and Hazel. 'You two are comin' with me.'

They scurried, avoiding his toecaps, and eventually it was time to say goodbye. Strain and privation choked their voices, their embraces were brief, for the scrap man had no tolerance of love. Looking down on them from the wagon seat he raged, 'Get a bloody move on.'

His paltry needs and wants. Lily didn't get a move on but in a tauntingly slow manner finished packing her own belongings, finally lifting Hazel onto the wagon and climbing in after her. The scrap man said, 'About time,' and clicked his tongue at Irish and then they were creaking down the track. As always, Lily felt bereft and sullen, as though she were leaving an essential part of herself behind. She looked back: the stone house, the fowl house, Wife and Big Girl receding from view. Not wanting to infect Hazel with her sadness, she settled a neutral expression on her face, let her mind drift, and so the hours unfolded, taking them further into the back country again.

pestilence

EVENING FELL, THE SKY HUNG WITH STARS, AND WHEN THE
moon came sailing above the plains it was ringed with a
spooky light. Everything seemed queer to Lily: the events
of the day, the swirling air. There was going to be rain.
Meanwhile the scrap man started drinking, draining two
sherry bottles and tossing them into the stony grass, where
they shattered and caught the icy moon glow. Drunk, he was
prone to all kinds of miscalculations and Lily was about to tell
him to stop for the night when his chin fell to his chest and
he sagged against her shoulder, a dead weight. She grabbed
the reins, and at the first likely roadside clearing, called Irish
to whoa, and so they camped.

The sky grew in rumbling torment after dark, lit by
lightning flares, with rising winds and sheets of rain. They
were dry inside the canvas hood but the air was thick,
scented by the scrap man's leaching alcohol, stale breath
and raw guts.

•

LILY OPENED THE flap with relief the next morning, letting a transfiguring breeze course around her. It lifted her spirits, chased the staleness away. And looking back into the dimness of their cave she saw Hazel smiling at her, even though somehow the scrap man had folded himself around her overnight. Rosalind was clasped to Hazel's chest, Hazel to the scrap man's, his arm flung over her torso – but he hadn't messed with her, just rolled against her. Yet many weeks stretched ahead. It was Lily's pure conviction that she could not let her guard down, not once.

She beckoned with a smile. 'Scrambled eggs?'

Last year the scrap man had swapped a dozen stolen plough-shares for a little kerosene stove, and as Lily melted dripping in a dented frying pan, Hazel wriggled free and perched beside her, slim and heedless, and together they cooked and ate.

The scrap man slept through the morning and, unregistered by him, the girls drove the wagon to the three farmhouses scattered along that long silent road. Old houses, but new to Lily. She was certain they'd never travelled this neck of the woods before.

She was used to the ways of isolated farm people, mired in suspicion of strangers, but this time something was different. At the first house the farmer held up a warning hand: 'Keep your distance.'

Lily was puzzled.

He hooked one hand to the braces that held up his pants, shielded his nose and mouth with the other. 'Don't come closer than six feet.'

'Old rags,' Lily said. 'Bottles, tins, scrap metal. Would your wife like a cheese grater or a coathanger?'

He considered that. 'Don't youse girls get off that wagon, you hear? Stay right there and I'll be back.'

He disappeared into his shed and emerged with a dented zinc bucket. Rather than bring it to them, he placed it on the ground. Stepped back, still covering his face. 'You can have it for free. I don't want to buy anything.'

Lily hopped down, tossed the bucket onto the tray, where it landed with a metal clatter that overrode the scrap man's snores.

The farmer said, 'Is that your father in there?'

She climbed aboard. 'Yes.'

'Letting you do all the work.'

Lily shrugged.

'Is he sick?'

'No.'

He turned to Hazel, opened his mouth as if to ask why she wasn't at school, but Lily cut him off. 'Thank you. Goodbye.'

He was in her mental map now. She didn't need a stone at the gate to catalogue him.

At the second house they were met by an old woman wearing a black dress, dusty on the shoulders, maybe from years in a wardrobe. A tall, fierce, erect, unequivocal woman who cried, 'Did you bring the pestilence with you?'

This was a morning for bewilderment. 'I beg your pardon?'

The woman tugged at her black sleeve. Behind her the farmhouse crouched mute beneath some towering gums and one ragged palm tree. There was no sense of the rhythms of farm life, no dogs, no men in big old gaping trousers, no sheep or spluttering tractor, no fresh tillage of the soil or green shoots appearing. A dying place.

'I lost my husband to it,' the woman said with glittering eyes, ravaged with emotions.

Lost him to what? 'So sorry,' Lily said.

Pouches of disapproval appeared around the woman's mouth. 'God's punishment for the spread of paganism, that's what it is.'

At the third house there was a leashed dog and grass-cropping sheep in the paddock beside the main shed, their jaws fairly tearing at the green. Revealed on the damp soil of the narrow yard was a tracery of spindly tyre tracks, which Lily read as a car reversing from the shed and heading out to the road. No one answered her knock at the door and the door was locked. Shopping? Visiting the doctor? Was today Sunday?

Lily fetched Hazel down from the wagon and they circled the house, trying the other doors, and all was still and silent and shut against the world. Except for one tiny window high above the ground at the rear. Partly open, and with a one, two, three, Lily boosted Hazel up to the gap. Hazel pushed, the window slid higher, and with a flip of her heels she was inside. The minutes passed and Lily's heart beat and the floors creaked and Hazel's face was at the window, creased in smiles. She reversed out, Lily caught her and now they were richer by a ten-shilling note, a lady's watch and pearl earrings. A rusty axe-head in the shed, a length of angle iron, two fencing droppers they could barely lift aboard the wagon.

This time the clatter woke the scrap man. He stood with his air of a man only partly finished by God and pissed over the side of the wagon. The damp soil received his dampness. He belched and asked them where they were.

•

THE NEXT DAY they rolled through the old goldfields country near Bendigo, a region of forgotten gullies and rudderless hope, coming to a town set on a branch line. As they trundled from one end to the other, Lily saw no friendly faces, barely any faces at all. It was the kind of town that might seem blurred and disfigured even to those who lived there, no matter how vivid the daylight, and today was crystal clear after the storm.

But here on the outskirts was a scrap yard with a shed and a loading dock beside the railway line. They knocked, no answer, knocked again, and finally stepped in, finding long reaches of empty floor and echoes in the dark corners. A few piles of fencing wire and angle iron and two tight bales of smelly rags. Dust. Their own footprints in the dust, tracking over those left by small creatures.

'The bastard must of gone out of business,' the scrap man said, quite lost.

They trooped out and a police constable stood beside the wagon, a white mask around his lower face. Smiling tormentedly, the scrap man nevertheless hissed at Lily from the side of his mouth, 'You girls get in the wagon,' before calling in a jolly voice: 'Hello there. Mr Carter said if I was ever passin' I should call in and he'd give me a good price but he must be on holiday.'

A fly droned disconsolately from the shed door, veering towards the policeman. He swiped at it, his eyes dark and knotted. 'I regret to inform you Mr Carter passed away.'

'Oh dear. His heart, was it?'

'The flu,' said the policeman, the mask deadening his voice.

'The flu?' echoed the scrap man.

The policeman couldn't believe his ears. His brow creased in irritation. 'The Spanish flu.'

'Oh,' said the scrap man, none the wiser.

'The *epidemic*,' said the policeman, still frowning. 'Millions dead around the world. Have you been asleep all this time?'

Pretty much, thought Lily. And she understood, now, everyone's strange behaviour.

'Six dead right here in this district,' the policeman was saying. '*Six*, including Bob Carter.'

He seemed bitterly fulfilled by the statistic and took a few steps back from the scrap man as though to escape infected air. 'You must wear a mask. It's irresponsible not to. Are you so indifferent to the lives of those helpless little girls?'

Lily clamped her hand over her nose and mouth, nudged Hazel. Hazel, dreamy with some things, quick with others, promptly covered her nose and mouth.

The scrap man needed to save face. 'I assure you we are clean-living people,' he said, full of affront and bluster.

'That might be so, but you and your daughters would do well to move on. You could be carrying the flu and we don't want any more sickness here. Go home.'

They left, rolling through the town. Lily saw a masked woman at the closed door of the grocer's, a basket over her arm, a shopping list in her hand. As she watched, the door opened a slit, a gloved hand snatched the list, the door closed again. The library was shut. A little cinema was closed until further notice. The pub was limiting patrons to five minutes. The scrap man, reading aloud all of these bewildering strictures, said blowed if he'd be coming back to *this* town any time soon. Passing a pharmacy, he hauled on the reins to peer through his red eyes at yet another sign in a window. '*Doctor*

Morse's Indian Root Pills,' he read. *'Recommended by medical men for the influenza and other complaints. Remarkable results.'*

He patted his pockets. They had no money.

•

MILLIONS DEAD AROUND the world was not a readily assimilated tragedy as far as the scrap man was concerned. Knowing full well they had nothing to show for this journey so far, and having fled from home poorly prepared, he had thoughts only of the next back-roads sucker, the next small-town scrap buyer. He said what he always said: 'Pull a long face and carry on.'

As they set up camp in a clearing amid pine trees late that afternoon, Lily listed their needs in her mind. They had a few eggs in danger of cracking, a few potatoes, a tin of tea-leaves, a packet of sugar and half-a-dozen dented tins of bully beef and vegetable soup. They badly needed more food, money, kerosene for the cooker. And beer or sherry for the scrap man. Nothing else kept him docile, and even that could not be guaranteed. She tipped two tins of soup into a pot and heated it through, one eye on the scrap man. No booze, a day of disappointments – a nasty heat was in him.

So after dinner she whispered to Hazel, 'Sleep under the wagon tonight.'

Hazel would hear them above her head and she would feel the cold ground beneath, but sooner that than attract the scrap man's eye.

Later, when the scrap man slept, Lily thought of running. Grab Hazel, saddle Irish, and flee. But where? How?

•

SORE AND STICKY in the morning, she washed at a puddle in the ditch beside the road. The water was brown but wet, cleansing, and her mood improved and she had tea made and eggs ready when Hazel emerged with Rosalind from the slab of shadow under the wagon. The first thing Hazel did was embrace her wordlessly. Her heart cracked from side to side.

They ate and let the scrap man sleep and rolled through the back country again. They earned no money that day. No one wanted to buy. They were given a few bits and pieces of scrap metal, that's all, and so it was the next day and the next. The changing skyline, the curving roads, the folds in the earth, the mix of densely wooded corners and tracts of emptiness, all resolved themselves on the sixth day into a road Lily recognised. They were nearing the town with the bluestone mill on the river. She woke the scrap man.

With three hours of daylight left, the scrap man took them straight to Morrison's Scrap Metal Bought and Sold in the shed beside the railway line. Morrison met them in his yard, keeping his distance but nonchalant with his mask, which dangled like a second chin beneath his large round face. Recognising Lily, he nodded hello. 'So you're back.'

Shivering in the chilly winds from the hills and the river, the scrap man gestured at the wagon. 'Got a load of stuff.'

Morrison glanced incuriously at the load, not bothering with a close look. He stroked his jaw lazily and said, 'Five bob.'

Lily read contempt in his voice and face. He had no time for a man who dragged his lasses around the countryside, where they might get sick.

And five shillings? Better than nothing, but it would last no time at all, especially if the scrap man drank it away. She was inclined to argue with Morrison, but she doubted it would do any good. Meanwhile the scrap man was miserably tempted. Five bob's worth of beer . . .

'Done,' he told Morrison, 'and I can bring you another load by the end of the week.'

Morrison shook his head. 'Won't do you any good. The trains are running on a restricted timetable because of the flu, and I've got a shedload of stuff that no one wants.'

Was this a story to be repeated from town to town? Lily thought so, but saw bafflement on the scrap man's face. She watched him walk up to Morrison with his hand out but the dealer, calmly tugging his mask over his nose and mouth, dodged away and tipped the money onto the tray of the wagon.

He kept back as the scrap man and the girls unloaded. As they climbed aboard the wagon again he said, 'Youse need masks.'

•

THEY FOUND THE bluestone mill unchanged and unoccupied. Lily, powerfully reminded of how evilly the walls and floor stored the chilly dampness, hunted around for kindling. Adding a couple of floorboards and a door lintel, she soon had a fire going, with no help from the scrap man, who unhitched and mounted Irish and cantered wordlessly off in search of a pub.

The first thing Lily thought was: Without Irish we can't escape.

Hungry now, she shook the kerosene tin, hearing only a faint sloshing. Enough to cook dinner and breakfast? It was not in the scrap man's reckoning to think they might run out of kerosene. It had happened before, but this time around Lily felt that the dimensions of their life were not limitless but contracting. Something was wrong in the world, the walls were closing in, life was unsupportable.

She found herself staring at Hazel. What was to happen to them?

Hazel must have sensed Lily's scrutiny. She turned, smiled reflexively, the smile fading when she saw Lily's intensity. She looked frightened.

Lily shook off her mood, gave Hazel a hug and went briskly about heating bully beef for dinner. They ate and chatted, Hazel a sunny presence again, and then the scrap man was back, baffled and outraged.

'It's the same everywhere! They kick you out after one beer. What's the world coming to?'

He paused, a calamitous realisation coming to him. 'Jesus Christ Almighty, I can't even send you kids in to pick pockets.'

Lily got some tea and bully beef into him quickly but she knew he'd want her later; he had very few ways to express or relieve his wretched provocations. So at bedtime she told Hazel to sleep under the wagon again. Hazel knew, clever thing: her goodnight hug was full of infinite sorrow.

•

NEXT MORNING THE girls walked Irish to the river to drink and to fetch water. Toting it back in a bucket, they heated it on the fire, then, looking about for peeping toms, stripped to nothing and sluiced away the accumulated filth of their days on the road. Hair first, lathered and rinsed, then every inch of every limb, scrubbed raw with soap and rags. It was a strange, twitchy, exhilarating half-hour, the air like razors, the water delicious, the soap stinging their eyes, the sensation afterwards of being unassailable.

Seeing the shivers in Hazel's skinny limbs, Lily gathered sunlight in the folds of her towel. 'Here,' she said, pouring it over her sister's astonished head.

'Let me,' urged Hazel, pouring sunlight over Lily.

Then they combed their wet locks and pulled on clean dresses and threw back their heads in vivid joy and walked into town while the scrap man slept.

At the first house a woman stood behind her flyscreen door and said, 'Yes?'

'Hello, me and my sister was wonderin' if you have any eggs to spare. Or milk. Bread. We just got here and our dad don't start his new job till tomorrow and –'

The woman said, 'Please step back off the veranda. I'll get you something but please step back off the veranda.'

They waited, Hazel's trusting hand in Lily's. They were two clean, combed sisters there on the woman's garden path. Hazel chattered brightly, not one given to communicating in grunts, and Lily listened. Half listened. She wondered what the woman was up to. Sneaking out the back way to alert the Social or the Education? And as they waited she felt again a queerness in her belly. She'd felt it yesterday, the day before, a fullness in her chest and a kind of contradictory warmth and slowness together with a keen attentiveness to smells, sounds, textures. And what she would give for an orange now, or chocolate.

She put the craving to one side when the screen door edged open a crack. The woman, masked, inched out a hand and settled a paper bag on the veranda. 'There you go. You girls had better move on now, hear? Careful who you run into. Remember to wear your masks in future.'

At the next house they were told to move on, at the third they were handed potatoes and a wrinkled apple.

More houses, more timid offerings, and sometimes anxiety and abuse. Wayfaring strangers welcomed by no one, they returned by way of the main street – and happened to see the scrap man, indignation on him as hands ejected him from a pub. Lily promptly grabbed Hazel and pulled her into the nearest shop.

A bell pinged above their heads. They were in a general store: tinned food, tools, clothing. Shock and silence greeted them. The shopkeeper and his customers – four women in overcoats, handbags hooked to their arms – wore masks. All five gaped at the girls. Finally the shopkeeper pointed a trembling finger. 'You know the rules.'

'Pardon?' said Lily.

'No congregating.'

Lily had no idea what he was talking about. And the blank masks, staring, immobile, frightened her badly. She sheltered Hazel behind her, didn't know what to do, didn't want to return to the footpath and encounter the scrap man.

'*No more than five persons may enter the shop at any one time,*' the shopkeeper said. 'Better still, tell your parents to post me their order. Slip it under the door. Or telephone.'

All eyes were hard and fierce. A woman said, 'Who are you, anyway? Why aren't you wearing your masks?'

Lily tried for disdain, nonchalance, but found herself hurrying Hazel out onto the footpath. No scrap man, thankfully, but she felt dispossessed, susceptible to everything.

•

Masks. They needed masks against germs. They needed masks to reassure potential customers.

Back at the wagon, Lily rummaged around for the flour bag in which she'd stored items that few people bought: table napkins, pillowcases, antimacassars. Fashioned by Big Girl's clumsy fingers from old bedsheets, they bore pinpricks of her blood here and there, if you looked closely. They bore the shadows of old stains. So thin they'd render into dust if looked at sideways.

At the bottom was a greyish pillowcase that Lily believed would never attract a customer. She held it to her face, made an approximate measurement – two hand-lengths in width, one in height – and cut three shapes. Finally, narrow strips for the straps, Hazel helping her stitch them in place.

As expected, the scrap man's first reaction was rage. 'Do you think we can afford to waste good material?' and 'Did I say you could do this?'

Lily drew herself up. She wanted to say, 'Use your brains,' but said, 'People won't have anything to do with us if we don't wear masks. They're scared we'll give them the flu.'

It sank in. He grumbled, to save face, and turned away to contemplate his meagre fire and empty bottles.

•

THEY TRAVELLED ON from the town, deeper into the back country, achieving some success in the untravelled regions, where the farms were far apart and the people not so well-informed or afraid. Even so, sales were sluggish. It was rare to see an acquisitive light come into the scrap man's eyes. Lily hid as much of their earnings as she could, knowing full well his miserable temptations. It helped that the pubs had their blasted five-minute rule.

The weeks passed. The accommodating farmhouses dried up and the scrap man and his girls lost the will to negotiate or even send Hazel in through a window. In the towns they were increasingly beset by hostility. Doors were slammed in their faces along the back streets and the main streets were ghostly, empty, apart from white-masked figures behind shop windows. Otherwise the only figures abroad were dogs, an occasional policeman or a limbless soldier on a park bench, lost in his greatcoat, his face seeking the meagre sun. These men would hear the wagon wheels creak and glance across, incurious and implacable. They had seen horrors on the battle-fields; a tinker and his wagon was not a horror, it was nothing.

And in the face of it all, the scrap man began to unravel. Baffled, uncomprehending, he would say, as another door slammed: 'We are ruined.' He spent their hard-won income on beer and cheap sherry and was often drunk now. No grand plans. He could barely string thoughts together. Forgot to look dapper and smilingly devilish to the ladies. In Lily's mind he was a shadowy, unfinished creature.

Curiously, her sense of strain and privation began to lift. Taking Hazel by the chin one day, she said, 'We are going home,' and turned the wagon around.

•

SHE WAS AFRAID, she was exhilarated. Home was perhaps weeks away and she could not rely on a drunken man to find the route across the uncertain plains. The days passed, the roads unfurled; then, bit by bit, she began to recognise familiar landmarks. These trees, towns, gateposts, shepherd huts and stone walls gave her hope – but not certainty. Sometimes she turned left when she should have turned right or not at all, but the time came when she knew that home was a day or two away. Even Irish sensed it. Years older now, he was apt to tire more quickly, but he could smell home; home was somewhere over that hill or around that bend.

If not steering by landmarks, and attempting some commerce at lonely farmhouses, Lily's hands were full with Irish, Hazel and the scrap man. Oats, water and short days for Irish. Stimulation for Hazel, who would shoot her bright gaze at the passing world, Rosalind in her hands, but was clearly sick of it all and was mostly silent. And cheer up the scrap man who, if not in a stupor, was sorry for himself. 'We're ruined,' he'd say. 'I'll have to sell the farm.'

He wanted to lash out at someone, anyone, and Lily always seemed to bait his hook. Hating her air of patience and containment, the way she sat with one hand on the reins, the other hand around Hazel's shoulders, he'd aim his bulky, affronted jaw at her and rage, or break into great bouts of sobbing and tell her she was nothing compared to his wife. And then he'd turn around and swamp Lily in the night. Lily, removed in reverie, dreamed of a home with Hazel and telling of her heartfelt love. She dreamed of whispering, 'Let's run away.'

'*If you run away again I'll kill you*,' was the scrap man's promise. Not if we get a head start, she thought.

At last they came to the long final trail to the stone hut, mist-blurred this morning, the sun too weak and low to burn it away. 'Home,' Lily said to the scrap man, who was slumped beside her, racked by a wet chesty cough, yet oddly touched with expectation. He turned on her his gentlest smile and agreed, 'Home.' Home would make it all better.

But home was barely welcoming. They reached the yard and there were the hens scratching about but no chimney smoke, no one materialising, and the old horse too dispirited to prick his ears. Lily stepped down from the wagon, lifted Hazel to the ground, helped the scrap man in his woozy descent, and still no one greeted them.

Hazel skipped across to the hut, a ripple of light in that dim place, her hair flying, Rosalind swinging from her hand. Reaching the doorstep, she stopped, jerked back, as if rebounding from invisible wires. She turned, seeking Lily's eyes, her thin face communicating doubts and agony, and then she took a step away from the house, and another.

Lily ran, the scrap man stumbling after her, to see what had befallen the household.

pouring the sun

death rustling

THE SCRAP MAN CLENCHED HIS FISTS. 'DID YOUSE TWO GET into the grog?' he demanded.

Wife sat in her wastes on the cold kitchen floor, her back against the wall, Big Girl's head in her lap. She was stroking Big Girl's slack cheeks and waxy forehead, over and over again, which Lily could see had done no good at all.

'Well?'

'Don't be stupid,' Wife told him, rattles in her throat.

The scrap man took a closer look, jerked away. 'She's dead,' he said, as if he'd uncovered a great truth hitherto concealed from him.

'Two, free days ago,' croaked Wife, continuing her stroking motions, a lost and lonely figure on the chilly floor.

Lily took charge, prodding the scrap man to go fetch firewood, urging Hazel to collect the eggs and walk Irish to his pen. When they were gone she dragged Wife free of the body, cut off her rags, cold-sponged her shivering bones and helped her into clean clothes and finally into bed. Returning to the kitchen, she emptied her mind and dragged Big Girl by the heels around to the storeroom. She was anachronistic, an obstacle, not Big Girl. This was a task, and her life was full of tasks. All Lily registered was the oddly malleable nature of this object, its surface dimpling from the pressure of her fingers. Then back to sluice and mop the kitchen floor and prod the scrap man into greater effort: 'Don't just sit there staring at the flames in the grate, make a pot of tea, heat up some soup.' In this way – keeping busy, issuing orders – Lily kept life going, for she could hear death rustling nearby. She had been hearing death for the past few weeks, she realised. They had not left death behind by coming home.

•

SHE DID NOT find a moment to sit until she took soup and hot sweet tea to Wife and helped her eat. 'Is that better?'

Wife coughed. 'Don't feel that good.'

Lily stroked Wife's face. Wife was burning up.

The scrap man had come to the doorway. Lily sensed him looking on, feeling left out. She paid him no mind.

He coughed to get her attention. 'We better dig a hole termorrer.'

Wife struggled to sit up. 'A proper burial.'

The scrap man ignored her. 'Over by the creek.'

Over by the creek was too stony. Everywhere was too stony on the scrap man's acres. Lily didn't say that but wiped Wife's chin and went in search of Hazel, who would have questions and had been overlooked since they got home.

•

THAT NIGHT LILY slept where Big Girl usually slept, beside Hazel in the dim, low-ceilinged middle room. It was her first night in a bed in a house. She did not count the draughty barns and mills of the past few years. Could she live in a house and never see the moon shadows or the play of the sun on the grass? She whimpered, feeling that the walls were closing in, and kept looking towards the door. Only Hazel calmed her, pressed hard against her back, heart beating, blood ticking, warm and comforting, until finally Lily fell asleep.

In the morning she added wood to the coals, heated water, fried some eggs. Driven by hunger, beckoned by the aromas of the kitchen, Wife appeared, slow and heavy after her days on the floor with a dead girl's head in her lap. She sat at the table, racked with the shivers, so Lily wrapped a coat about her shoulders.

'Should you be up?'

Wife didn't hear her. She stared at nothing, forehead glistening, and said, 'The baby was due any day.'

In her quick and subtle way, Lily plonked scrambled eggs and a cup of tea before Wife and bustled about the chilly room, stopping for an occasional hug of the woman's bony shoulders. Then Hazel wandered in, sleepy-eyed, bringing light. The scrap man continued to sleep in rattly torment down along the little hallway.

'I want her buried proper,' Wife said, spelling out her urgent truth again.

Buried proper did not mean a hole over by the creek. What did it mean?

Drawing on her years and wisdom, Wife said, 'Like in a cemetery and that. A priest to say a few words over her. A proper coffin and that.'

She shuffled back to bed. Lily sat and thought. A coffin, a cemetery, a priest . . . It all added up to expenses and the intervention of the authorities, so no wonder the scrap man was leery.

She came to a decision. Sending Hazel to fetch the face masks, she took a knife blade to the mud plug and prised out her nugget. She pulled on her best dress, coat and boots – poor, threadbare items passed down to her from Big Girl and Wife before her – and poked and tugged Hazel into shape. Finally the girls hitched Irish to the buggy and rode, masked, into town while the scrap man still slept.

The place was as blank-featured and devoid of life as anywhere else, but Lily, fearful of encountering a busybody like the farmer's wife, wasted no time in parking the buggy and slipping with Hazel into the bank. Her mask was itchy. It stank. But it reassured the teller, a man with sleek hair and tiny, nose-pinching glasses perched above his mask.

'Yes?'

His voice was muffled but the tetchiness shone through. Suffused with self-consciousness, Lily mumbled that she had a gold nugget for sale, did the bank buy gold?

'Did you steal it?'

That stung. Lily drew herself up. 'I did not. We found it on our property.'

The teller chewed on that. 'Why are you selling it?'

'My father died.'

The teller shrank from her. 'The flu?'

For the first time, Lily visualised the flu. A miasmic force, it lodged in you and moved on. Had it lodged in her? Hazel? She glanced down at Hazel, who gazed up at her, bright-eyed and buzzing with life.

But if the teller feared their proximity to death, he might kick them out. Lily shook her head adamantly and said, 'He fell off his horse.'

Tension left the teller. 'May I see the nugget?'

Lily fished it out, passed it across the counter. The teller picked it up with his handkerchief and tipped it onto a set of scales, adding tiny weights, watching one side go up, the other down. Finally, consulting a ledger, he quoted a price.

'That's what gold was fetching last week,' he said with a sniff. 'Unless Madam obliges me to telegraph Melbourne at her cost so that I might enquire as to the latest price?'

His tone said to do that was more trouble than it was worth. Lily shook her head.

'Very well,' he said, and, with an air of silky attention, he counted out her money: pound notes, ten-shilling notes, florins, shillings, sixpences and one lonely ha'penny.

•

'A PRIEST TO say a few words,' Wife had said.

Lily and Hazel traipsed all over town and found him beside a fresh grave at the cemetery on the hill. This was a place of weeds and lichened old headstones and a number of fresh new dirt mounds. The girls stood back respectfully and the wind moaned and the priest droned and a handful of people huddled against the wind and the death they could smell coming for them.

When he was done and the mourners had drifted away, Lily fronted up to him.

'My sister has died.'

'I see.'

'She needs to be buried proper.'

He looked down at her. 'Was she of the faith?'

What was he talking about? 'Buried proper,' Lily said, feeling uneasy yet stubborn in the face of a man all in black.

His face softened. No longer disobliging, he said, 'I have another burial today and two tomorrow.'

He gave a little cough and looked exhausted and close to death himself. Lily waited.

'This is most irregular,' he said, and still Lily waited.

'Two o'clock sharp,' he said eventually. He gestured at the scene behind him, the pallbearers dispersing and two men leaning on shovels. The wind rose mournful in the pine trees and clouds streamed across the sky, the shadows chasing along the ground. A scrappy bird attacked the priest but it was only a bit of newspaper that he swatted at. 'Two o'clock sharp,' he said, 'and a donation for my services.'

He nodded towards the gravediggers. 'And those men will need to be informed, and paid.'

•

BACK DOWN THE hill in the buggy, following Irish's weary, undulating spine through the town to the timber yard. According to the gravediggers, the nearest undertaker was miles away and snowed under, but the timber yard might do them a cheap pine box.

'Wood to make a coffin,' Lily told the timber merchant. 'For our sister.'

'How big?'

'Bigger than me.'

'Adult,' the man said. A wiliness creeping in, he took Lily and Hazel to a pile of planks. 'Take a look. Jarrah. Beautiful wood.'

'Pine,' said Lily.

'You sure? Jarrah will last ya.'

'Pine.'

'I can make it up this afternoon.'

Lily could feel the edge of his greed, but she had money in her pocket now and was not about to throw it away. 'We will take the wood with us and make it at home.'

He shook his head. 'You lassies drive a hard bargain.'

Still not saying he was sorry their sister had died, he went away with bad grace and returned with a few splintery pine planks. Lily paid and they began the long trek back to the stony acres, the girls walking, the pine boards balanced on the buggy seat.

They trudged up to the hut to find the scrap man awake and in a state of rage. 'Where the hell have you been?'

His fist caught Lily on the ear. The ear, already chilled by the wind, hurt like mad and when she got to her feet there was mud on her dress and tiny stone chips in both knees. 'Don't!' shrieked Hazel, sheltering Lily, and he sent her flying, too.

Then maybe it was Irish's turn but the pine boards stopped him. 'What's this?'

'To make a coffin with,' Lily said. Her ears were ringing.

'You paid good money for this?' he shouted.

'Stole it,' Lily said.

One of his monstrous glints came into his eyes. He liked to think he was one-up on everyone. His whole family, one-up on the rest of the world. 'That's my girl.'

He cast a crafty look at the wood. 'Pity to waste it on a coffin. Why don't you girls grab a shovel each and –'

'No!' said Wife, slow and drooping in the doorway. 'We do it proper.'

'We take care of our own in this family,' returned the scrap man.

Lily stared at him, and as she did, a great peace settled in her, her body unknotting. He was a little man, driven by paltry needs and deprivations. This was *her* family, not his. Poking his grimy shoulder she snarled, 'The priest said tomorrow at two. Do you want him to send the Social or the constable if we don't turn up?'

'Ah,' said the scrap man with a fed-up gesture and stomping off to the storeroom.

He returned with a saw, a hammer and rusty bent nails from old boards he'd scrounged over the years. Using the tray of the cart as a workbench, he sawed and hammered furiously until a passable coffin took shape. The effort stirred his phlegmy cough. 'There,' he said. 'Satisfied?'

•

THE NEXT DAY dawned with moody clouds again, rain on the winds. While Hazel fetched the eggs, spending busy time away from the house, the others carried Big Girl to the coffin on the back of the wagon. Big Girl was five days dead now. Dust to dust, ashes to ashes, a stink was on her. Lifting her, tumbling her into the coffin, was like wrestling a clammy sack of potatoes loosely packed. Even the scrap man was silenced by it.

Then it was time to leave but Wife had meanwhile changed her mind. In the kitchen with an onion, carrots and a cutting board she croaked that she had said her goodbyes. 'I will stay and cook the soup.'

Her face wore the ravages of time and a hardscrabble life, and something new, paleness and sweat and cheeks sharply etched. Lily didn't want to think about it but smiled and touched her forearm. At the door she looked back uneasily. Wife's eyes on her. Solemn, dark, wise eyes.

By two in the afternoon they were at Big Girl's hole in the ground above the town. The scrap man grew shifty to see a priest and gravediggers there, and looked about as if a policeman or the Education or the Social might appear. But there were no other observers, and as the priest intoned over the grave, stunned with exhaustion, little pity left for anyone, Lily held Hazel close against her side. The scrap man? The scrap man stood back wringing his hands, in a hurry to leave.

When it was over, the scrap man scurrying to the cart, Lily pressed coins into the hands of the priest and the gravediggers. Now the long drive back, the three figures silent, a soughing wind and the plodding hooves the only sounds, until there was the stone hut and Wife dead on her mattress and so they would have to do it all over again.

●

THE FIRST THING Lily did was hurry Hazel back to the kitchen. She crouched before the child. 'Do you feel sick?'

Hazel coughed experimentally, shook her head, gave Lily a gap-toothed grin. But life had become perilous on the stony acres so Lily scrutinised her closely. Pink cheeks. Bright eyes. A sense of thrumming life.

With some misgivings Lily stood, gave Hazel a little shove and said, 'Gather the eggs, feed the horses, fetch some kindling.'

'Is she dead too?' Hazel asked, peering past Lily's shoulder.

'Yes.'

Hazel pondered that a while. She skipped away.

Lily turned to the scrap man. As if she might be concerned for his health, he thumped his chest. 'Fit as a fiddle.'

Buggered if she cared. Her mind was on the priest, the gravediggers, and did they have enough pine boards.

Almost no money left.

The scrap man sought her attention again. Screwing a sorrowing look onto his face he said, 'It's just us now, girlie.'

As if grief bound them together, the three of them against the world, but Lily knew he was not grieving. And he was indifferent to her grief. Nothing about him ever rang true, except rage and self-pity. *Two less mouths to feed*, that's all the emotion he'd be feeling.

She stared at him. Discomfited, he turned away, plonked himself at the kitchen table, and Lily walked through to the room where Wife lay dead. Reluctant to enter, she hesitated at the doorway, thinking of the next few hours, the next few days.

Suddenly the scrap man was pressing against her in a humid, greasy embrace, snivelling that she was his best girl. 'Just us now.'

Lily was through with all of that. 'We need to move her to the storeroom.'

'What are we to do?' cried the scrap man.

'*Move her to the storeroom.*'

Denied consolation, he pushed past Lily sulkily and stood at Wife's feet. 'Get a move on then, grab her shoulders.'

Wife was not yet cold, Lily could scarcely bear it, but the thought of sleeping in the hut with Wife close by was more than she could endure. They manoeuvred Wife around to the storeroom, placed her on her back, folded her arms across her chest. Lily cried now. Wife was not so bad.

'How about we bury this one here instead of the cemetery.'

'No,' said Lily.

The scrap man tried for helpless longing. 'I just want her close by.'

'*No.*'

'All right, all right, just sayin'.'

Lily stormed back to the kitchen, needing the warmth from the stove. She pulled a chair up, sat a while, at a loss. She wanted nothing but to sleep after her mad rushing around. But she was afraid to sleep, for she might not wake. Was she sick, like the others? She took her senses to all the corners of her body, testing, searching. Not sick. But she did have a strange fullness low in her torso; she'd been feeling queer alterations for days. A warm, slow, budding contentment.

The scrap man wandered in. He began turning things over, cups and plates and pots and pans. He poked his dirty paws in the tea tin, pulled out drawers, looked under the sink.

'Don't just sit there, help me look.'

Lily ignored him.

'Help me look, damn it.'

'For what?'

'She was a great one for hidin' money.'

Lily stood, fighting fatigue and the new, slow expansiveness of her body. 'I need to do dinner.'

'That can wait. You look in the bedroom.'

Lily quickly found a pound note, three ten-shilling notes and a handful of florins and shillings inside Wife's box of monthly rags. Stuffing the paper money and four florins into her boots, she walked through to the kitchen with the remaining coins in her hand.

'Found it.'

She tipped the coins onto the table. The scrap man swooped. 'Told you!'

•

AFTER BREAKFAST THE next morning, Lily readied Irish for the ride to town. More pine boards, her mental list said. The priest. The gravediggers.

She called Hazel. Called again. Still no Hazel, so she checked the fowl house, the yard, the hut, finding Hazel in the kitchen, seated with the scrap man, who had manacled her forearm with his grimy claw.

He gave Lily one of his sly looks. 'Keepin' the girl here. Don't want you runnin' off on me. If you run off, I'll do her in, understand?'

Laziness, anger and self-pity had always been his greatest talents. And reading your mind, twisting the knife. Lily stiffened. 'Don't you dare touch her.'

The scrap man waved that aside. 'This is what's gonna happen. Soon as the wife's in the ground, I'm sellin' her old nag and youse two are gonna work flat out sewin' and jam makin', all right?'

Lily rode off, Wife's money in her boot. Life would go on. He would have wives, there would be babies, his womenfolk would make useless goods to sell. He will never die. I will die. He will leave me to die and travel the backblocks with

Hazel. Hazel will wither and die, but I won't be around for it. Her children will wither and die . . .

Irish stumbled. He'd been overworked for year upon year, and so many return journeys to town in the past few days.

Flee with Hazel on foot, thought Lily. But he would hunt us down.

•

THE NEXT AFTERNOON, Wife in the ground, the scrap man locked the girls in the storeroom and boarded up the window.

'Food and water for a couple of days, mattress, what more do you want?' he rasped on the other side of the door, his coughing a wet thing in his chest.

'Where you goin'?'

'Sell the old nag,' he said. 'Be back before you know it.'

With money in his pocket he might be days. The hours passed, the night, another day. Lily was fearful but could not infect Hazel with it, so she told stories. She taught Hazel to sing a song of sixpence. Unfortunately four-and-twenty blackbirds baked in a pie was more than the child could contemplate. Hazel screwed up her face as if tasting bones, claws and feathers, and her bad feeling bled into claustrophobia and panicky tears.

'Hush,' soothed Lily. 'It will be all right, he'll be back soon.'

They wanted him back to let them out but they didn't want him back.

•

IN THE MORNING after their second night Irish came clopping into the yard, except it wasn't Irish and, before Lily could stop her, Hazel was shouting, 'You can let us out now.'

'Hello? Who's in there?'

Lily peered through a gap in the storeroom door. The Education on his horse. He dismounted neatly and knocked, a rather silly thing to do.

'Who's there?'

'Hush,' whispered Lily to Hazel.

'No one,' Hazel told the door.

The Education said, 'Dear, oh dear,' and strode off and came back with an iron fencing dropper. He inserted the pointy end and the window boards screeched, groaned, popping free of the scrap man's rusty nails. Light poured in. He removed his face mask and cupped his eyes against the glass, peering through the murky cobwebs and dust. The girls, nowhere to hide, were right where he could see them, hemmed in by boxes of useless stuff.

'Keep clear,' he shouted, and set about smashing the glass, the frame, finally folding his coat over the jagged shards so they could climb out.

'Lily,' he said, when she and Hazel had drained his waterbag, 'I have received reports, people have seen you in town.'

Lily was mute and feeble-minded but he went on: 'And

now this. Godfather. The authorities will have to be notified. If I had any say in it, you'd both be made wards of the state.'

Lily said nothing. Hazel, noting that, also said nothing.

'Where is everyone?'

Nothing.

'How long have you been locked up?'

Nothing.

'Did your father lock you up? I'll have to report him.'

He didn't wait for a reply but dropped his interrogatory voice and put his arm around them. 'Poor little mites, I'm told you had *two* deaths in the family.'

They were silent. Releasing them at last, he was all action. 'Right,' he said, clapping his hands, 'I want you both to stay here while I make arrangements. I'll be back very soon.'

He mounted his horse, gazed at them uneasily. Lily gazed back. He was clean, he smelled of leather and soap and the oil combed through his hair. He was a truly polished man where the scrap man tried to be and would always fail. But the Education was not her friend.

When they were alone she said, 'Quick.'

•

THEY FLED FROM the stony acres, their belongings, bundled in sugar bags tied with twine, bouncing against their spines. Across the dry creek and up the bank and along it, the back way to one of the district's little-used roads. Past the traps rusting in the grass, rabbit carcasses desiccating. That part of Lily's life was over with, and everything else the scrap man had in mind. If he was in a grip of selling, he might sell her, or Hazel. Why did my family sell me? Lily wondered. Was I not wanted? An old hazy picture swam into her mind, the house in the clearing, the pressing scrub and the mother, father and too many mouths to feed. Desperation and closed horizons and no one paying attention, that's how she got sold.

The Education had paid attention, but what did he want? He did not want two girls. In all of his kindness he nevertheless would not be saying, 'Come home with me.' Wards of the state, he'd said, and Lily didn't think that sounded much like a home or salvation.

She had a mind to find her brother. Head north-east to that town where the band played, where boys threw stones, and see if she could pick up his trail. If he had returned from the war. If he was her brother.

Lily and Hazel found a barn for the night and hanging from a rusty nail a canvas waterbag, which they filled from a stock trough. Dinner was horse carrots and a knuckle of bread, all they'd had time to pack, and some time before dawn, crippling cramps woke Lily, more powerful than her monthlies, with blood and clotted blood and no one to explain it.

•

MORNING CAME AND they carried on, an ache down low in Lily's belly. Bush tracks, never main roads. If they heard hooves or a buckboard motor they ducked behind fences and trees. Hazel did not complain, she was utterly trusting, but, like Lily, footsore and famished. Or we catch the train, thought Lily, hearing a distant choofing sometimes, a mournful whistle. She pictured a silent carriage with people staring over their face masks at the ragamuffins who'd had the nerve to travel alone, where were the parents, someone should inform the authorities.

She had no answers, and was still doubling over with cramps although the bleeding had stemmed, and she felt so addled right then that she began to weep, even as Hazel was saying in wonder, 'Lily, look, is that Irish?'

They rounded a bend in the track, came to a hollow beside a shallow creek, and it *was* Irish, cropping the roadside grasses, reins dragging, saddle on the ground. No scrap man.

Steal Irish and flee – but they could not do that. Up and down the creek the girls roamed, calling, 'Cooee,' and, 'Hello,' finally stumbling on the scrap man beside a pool of water trodden greenish-black by cattle. Who would want to drink it? Only a desperate man, and he'd fallen before he reached it, one hand outstretched. He was shivering uncontrollably, half wrapped in Irish's saddle blanket.

'Is he dying?' whispered Hazel.

His eyes opened, saw Lily crouched beside him. 'My best girl.'

His chest rattled, he was skin over bones. Lifting his chin, he saw Hazel. 'And the little one,' he croaked.

'Hazel,' said Hazel.

A great shudder went through him and he said he couldn't get warm. 'Take me home.'

Lily looked across at Irish. However would they hoist the scrap man onto his back? Full of doubts, she went to fetch the horse, patting his neck to calm his snorts and whinnies. She grabbed the reins, led him along the creek to the scrap man – and what on earth was Hazel doing?

Some kind of awkward dance, elbows out, tilting the saddle blanket in the bowl of her arms. 'This will mend you,' she was saying in a singsong voice. 'Me and Lily do this when we get the shivers.'

The scrap man accepted the sunshine pouring over him as if it were his last chance. On his back now, he seemed to levitate.

Crouching, Lily said, 'Can you get up?'

'Don't feel good.'

Lily eyed the sky. Clouds were massing in the south but just now the day was windless, drenched in sunlight. She took the blanket from Hazel and spread it over the scrap man's croaky chest. He closed his eyes but his hand found hers, gripping powerfully as if work-toughened, not that he had ever worked; he was afraid, that was all.

'Thirsty,' he whispered.

She dribbled water into his mouth from her waterbag. The sun came in strong and warm and the girls stayed with him and he smiled and in a short while the smile froze in place. Irish gave a little trembling sidestep but presently settled, snatching at the grass with his big tombstone teeth, waiting for the girls to say goodbye. Emptied the scrap man's pockets and said goodbye, that's what they did.

GARRY DISHER

HER

Reading Group Notes

Questions for Discussion

1. The opening scene in the novel depicts a family with no hope, visited by a man with no scruples – a lethal and desperate combination. Discuss.

2. This narrative is, by its nature and authorial intent, emotionally cryptic. For example, we are never made privy to the mother's reaction to her husband's sale of their child; much later, Lily captures the eye of a young soldier and thinks that she recognises him as a brother. These are two of the many strands of this ambiguously suggestive narrative which are left to the reader to surmise. What other ideas or events are ambiguous in this novel?

3. We often hear of the social disintegration of contemporary society and how vulnerable people are victimised and left powerless and alienated. Coupled with this is a romanticised view of the past that endows those who lived then with 'traditional' values. Such views are ahistorical: how much more vulnerable were children and women 100 years ago when there were few social services, and no media coverage to report on family atrocities? This novel is a shocking indictment of adult abusers like the scrap man who took advantage of those who were young, powerless and vulnerable. Lily, Big Girl and Wife were all children when

he purchased them; Hazel is, horrifyingly, born into this family. This novel corrects the gap in historical narratives by focusing on the plight of these voiceless children. Discuss.

4. The scrap man is such a violent and abusive man; he appears to have no redeeming features. Might he too, though, be the victim of his upbringing?

5. Discuss the manner of the social welfare and education officers who visit the Stony Acres:

   The fine man dismounted and removed his own hat and offered a handshake. The scrap man stared at it dumbfounded but, quick to know what side his bread was buttered on, closed his mouth with a click of ill-fitting teeth, smiled, wiped his fingers on the slope of his trousers and said, 'Pleased to make your acquaintance.' (p 11)

   Do they really take any responsibility for these children, or are they simply adhering to an ineffectual code of practice?

6. This story takes place in a momentous historical period during which millions died in World War One, closely followed by the Spanish flu epidemic. And yet the characters seem oblivious to such crises. Is poverty and desperation a deterrent to historical awareness?

7. Underpinning this narrative is a rich social history seen through an historian's eye. Disher carefully weaves in a number of dying arts to paint a picture as deftly as any history book might do – the characters' chores, such as trapping and skinning rabbits; and their handicrafts, such as making toasting forks or creating clothes from flour bags and cooking jams and chutneys. Discuss what life was like, particularly for women in these times, living in such primitive conditions.

8. It is painful to read some parts of this narrative, so blatantly cruel are these people to each other:

   When they were satisfied that Lily wouldn't die, could walk, no broken bones, Wife said, 'That will do you. Now I want you to help with the sewin'.' (p 46)

   How does Lily survive such indifference?

9. Despite the bleakness of this narrative, it is peppered with lyrical tributes to the glories of the bush that offer sustenance to Lily:

   It was early spring, the grass all about thick and vivid, full of vigour and nodding with wildflowers. Birds carried nest-building mud and twigs in their beaks, ducks pecked and squabbled, kookaburras called and the days were longer and milder. (p 90)

Discuss the picture that the novelist paints of the landscape at various points in the novel and how it sometimes offers a little relief from the otherwise unrelenting desolation.

10. One of the grim messages in this novel is how evil may be passed on by a 'carer' to those in their 'care':

Lily would have a silent laugh. She knew all of his crooked ways, and she'd been reading him forever. Reading the mugs, too, seeing their pity. And distaste, as if her feeble-mindedness were catching. When that happened the mugs were just as likely to turn the scrap man away as buy from him, but he wasn't canny enough to see it. (p 53)

Discuss the idea that Lily is well on her way to becoming as crooked as the scrap man, when she is mercifully released from his clutches.

11. It is hard to believe that Lily might actually desire the scrap man's approbation, but she has been in his care for so long that she is literally trapped by his expectations:

Self-pity and a curious kind of jealousy shot through her to think she'd be replaced. (p 57)

Is she likely to be able to wrest herself from such emotional insecurity, later in life?

12. What might Lily's and Hazel's fates be now that they are entirely alone? Might the tough skills they've developed stand them in good stead? Or are they too damaged to lead successful lives?

Points on Writing Style for Discussion

Garry Disher's literary style is evident here in spare, beautifully crafted sentences rich with lyrical descriptive detail and literary devices. For example:

The ants streamed from holes that were like pores in the skin of the world. (p 14)

A collection of angles that did not fit with one another. Lumpy roundness, twiggy limbs, the square window a kind of tilted sail. (p 26)

Emotions are often conveyed by suggestive description as well:

She began to sift through the rags, her quick, assessing fingers testing seams and tensile strength. And there at the centre of one bundle was a tight red ball.

> *A dress.*
>
> *It seemed to sigh in relief as she shook it, to fill with air, shimmer and dance. It was corduroy, thick, warm. It had never been repaired or even needed repair. The red was the redness of a dark red rose. Mine, thought Lily. She had never owned a dress that was not once a grain sack.* (p 72)

Choose a particularly lyrical description to discuss.

Irony, sarcasm and black humour undercut the themes and the terrible tragedy that unfolds in this novel. For example:

> *But what she wanted to do more than anything was hit the Kaiser.*
>
> *A man in a bowler hat, vest and bow tie shouted, 'Do your bit for the boys at the front — knock the Kaiser off his perch.'* (p 116)

Lily has no idea who the Kaiser is, or what his part in the war is, so this is a slyly ironic passage.

And the humour is dark in this reference to the scrap man and his sexual predation:

> *Another day, another town, another bend in the road where a trooper might lie in wait — no wonder he was a man who every night had needs.* (p 121)

And Morrison, the scrap metal salesman, does not understand that Lily and Hazel have much worse than illness to
contend with.

> Lily read contempt in his voice and face. He had no time
> for a man who dragged his lasses around the countryside,
> where they might get sick. (p 164)

How does such bleak humour enhance the themes of this
novel?

**An effective narrative depends for its impact on carefully
honed syntax and cadence, and *Her* opens with a stunning
piece of text:**

> Out in that country the sun smeared the sky and nothing
> ever altered, except that one day a scrap man came by with
> his wife, who had cost him twelve shillings once upon a
> time, and a wispy girl, who had cost him ten.
>
> The people of the hut heard them first, the clop two
> three four of hooves, the creature-in-torment shriek of an
> axle and a mad symphony of tocking and rattling. They
> froze. Then, from the scrub line, came a bony horse, a
> wagon hung with pots and pans, a dog panting along in
> the lurching shade and three faces, dusty and gaunt.
>
> 'Whoa!' said the man, spying the hut and hauling on
> the reins.

The dust settled over the clearing. The pots and pans
fell silent on their hooks. The horse hung its head and the
dog belly-flopped onto the dirt. (p ix)

There is not a word wasted here; the descriptions ('smeared' or 'creature-in-torment shriek of an axle') are evocative, and the scene for the whole novel is set powerfully and atmospherically. Choose another particularly concise and suggestive passage and discuss how it is crafted and how it impacts on the reader.

Characterisation is conveyed via deft word pictures, for example:

The farmer removed his hat to think. A tidemark of grease
ringed the hatband. His dome, balding, was mottled and
pinkish under strands of hair combed back from a stark
white forehead. The rest of him was sun-darkened and
work-stained. Worn leather braces held his gaping pants
at chest height. He was unlovely. (pp 53–4)

Choose another character description and discuss how it presents that person.

Compare this novel to other such writing. Seek out collections of Australian classic short stories about battlers, such as Henry Lawson's *The Drover's Wife*, or classic 'road' novels.

Suggested Further Reading

Read some of Garry Disher's historical works for children and adults, for example:

Disher, Garry. *The Apostle Bird,* Hodder, 1997.
Disher, Garry. *The Bamboo Flute,* Hachette, 1992.
Disher, Garry. *The Divine Wind,* Hachette, 1998.
Disher, Garry. *Past the Headlands,* Allen&Unwin, 2001.
Disher, Garry. *The Stencil Man,* Collins, 1988.

See also Australian classic 'road' stories in the HarperCollins Classics series such as:

Cleary, Jon. *The Sundowners,* HarperCollins, 2013.
Cusack, Dymphna and Florence James. *Come in Spinner,* HarperCollins, 2013.
Johnston, George. *My Brother Jack,* HarperCollins, 2013.
Keneally, Thomas. *The Chant of Jimmie Blacksmith,* HarperCollins, 2013.
Langley, Eve. *The Pea-Pickers,* HarperCollins, 2013.
Tennant, Kylie. *The Battlers,* HarperCollins, 2013.

See also:
Park, Ruth. *The Harp in the South,* Penguin Modern Classics, 2009.
White, Patrick. *The Tree of Man,* Vintage Classics, 2011.

GARRY DISHER grew up on a wheat and wool farm in South Australia. He has an MA in Australian History and has lived, worked and travelled in England, Italy, Israel, the USA and southern Africa. In 1978 he was awarded a creative writing fellowship to Stanford University, California, where he wrote his first collection of short stories. Garry worked as a writing lecturer between the years 1980 and 1988, before becoming a full-time writer. He has published more than fifty books, including short story collections, literary novels, writers' handbooks and award-winning crime thrillers and children's titles. His website is:

garrydisher.com

hachette
AUSTRALIA

If you would like to find out more about Hachette Australia,
our authors, upcoming events and new releases you can visit
our website or our social media channels:

hachette.com.au

HachetteAustralia

HachetteAus

HachetteAus

HachetteAus